AMERICAN MONSTERS

MICHAEL SCHUSSLER JR

RAVEN TALE
PUBLISHING

Copyright © 2024 by Michael Schussler Jr

Published by Raven Tale Publishing

ISBN: 9798880395187

✳ Created with Vellum

To my family and friends, especially MM, ZS, and TG: Thank you for your undying support.
And to you, dear reader: May your monsters be contained.

PROLOGUE

July 13, 1966 ~ Evening

IT WAS one of those early summer evenings where the hot air from the day seems to float up into the sky as the sun begins to set, and the cool air from the ground below seeps out, icing away the summer sweat from the hours before.

Little Billy Callaway loved such evenings. He was speeding down the streets of Burnwell, West Virginia on his Schwinn Stingray, stand-style, feet pressing hard against the silver pedals, butt in the air hovering over the faded seat, chest and shoulders leaning out over the handlebars. It was an old bike, but a good one. It had been his older brother Mikey's until Mikey had gotten his driver's license last year and gotten bored with it. And every day since the school year ended and summer break began, 12-year-old Billy had been on that bicycle prancing about the town like a newly homed puppy hellbent on taking charge of his territory.

But as eager as Billy was to grind those bike tires down to the gears in the daylight, it was now getting dark, and quickly. Sun setting behind him, Billy pedaled faster than he ever had before, kicking up dust in the trail of his tires when he maneuvered between street and sidewalk.

For all the freedoms his parents had allowed him that summer with his new, hand-me-down bike, his father was very clear about one specific rule: BE HOME BEFORE DARK. NO MATTER WHAT.

"No matter what," Billy had echoed in the driveway earlier that day before racing off to join his friends at the park. But that promise now seemed impossible to keep. He'd cut it close a few times already this summer, rolling in with five or so minutes to spare before the sun fully set, his mom setting the table for supper. She looked at him with her hands on her hips those few times he was almost late, "You're lucky, mister. Good thing your father is working late or he'd ring your neck."

He would, too... Billy had no doubts about that. His father was a decent man, good as far as Billy knew. But the spankings could be frequent, especially when his father had been drinking, and a full-blown beating never seemed out of the question, though it was Billy's mother who usually got the brunt of that.

But Billy's father provided. He worked long, 12-hour shifts in the coal mines and never complained about the expenses. Mikey's new car, Billy's new baseball glove, Mommy's new record player (his father had smashed the old one in a fit of rage after his mother "forgot about the roast in the oven"). "A working man needs to eat!" his father screamed. Though judging by his father's monstrous gut, Billy guessed a working man could go a week without food and survive, maybe a month. "How's a miner get that fat anyway?" Billy's friends would sometimes tease. "How does he fit in there?" But for all the things his father might have been, a liar he was not. And when he promised Billy he'd be sorry if he got home after dark, Billy had understood that he would indeed be sorry if that were to happen.

He fully intended to be home before dark, but the backyard

baseball game he'd been playing with his friends had gone into extra innings. The score was tied 13-13, Billy was up to bat for the sixth time. He'd gone 1-5 on the day with 3 strikeouts (*good thing Dad isn't here to see this performance*, he thought.) But with 2 outs, a runner on third, and down in the count with 1 ball, 2 strikes, Billy had stripped a slider on a line over the shortstop's head, the runner on third scored easily and the game was over. Billy had won it. But in the thrill of the victory, the ecstasy of the celebration, Billy hadn't noticed how fast the sun was setting. To his friends' dismay, Billy had cut the celebration short, and rode off into the sunset toward home, leaving a barrage of cheers and whistles from his teammates drifting faintly in the distance.

"Billy the Bomber comes through in the clutch!" he shouted into the wind, the cool breeze nearly blowing his hat off as he turned the corner of his street. His house was at the far end of the block on the corner. From here he could see his brother Mikey in the driveway washing his car for what Billy guessed must have been the third time this week.

"Mikey! Guess WHAT!" Billy yelled from 200 yards away, still pedaling like a madman. Mikey looked up, but didn't holler back, he could guess exactly what if that boy wasn't in the house in 30 seconds. Mikey looked toward the setting sun, shook his head, and went back to scrubbing the windshield.

Billy was laughing, flying along the street, so close to home he could relax and catch his breath, his father would have to understand. Heck, he'd probably even be *proud* of Billy for having the game winning hit. So, he stopped pedaling and let the wheels glide along, still moving at a fairly rapid pace. He sat back down on the seat and looked behind him at the sun, now barely visible over the horizon. And that's when he saw it...

In the faint glow of the setting sun against the sky, Billy saw something standing on the roof of the house he was passing. He thought it looked like something from one of his *Batman* comics, like a gargoyle on the edge of a Gotham city skyscraper, or perhaps the caped crusader himself, perched on the top of a bridge scanning for crime. But as Billy rolled slowly by, his tires losing momentum now, he saw the head of the thing turn, and Billy realized this was no statue. Its red eyes followed him, and Billy craned his neck to the side, unable to look away, his bike humming lazily along the sidewalk. It was as if he *couldn't* look away. As if something terrible was going to happen if he did. Then Billy had the strangest feeling. He felt that perhaps he should not go home. That *home* was where the terrible thing was. And that as scary as this perched gargoyle seemed, it did not wish to harm him. But something else did...

Then Billy's front tire hit something hard, and he was flown from his seat, his ribs slamming into the handlebars, and his face smashing against a tree that stood near the sidewalk. He hit the ground hard, his bike falling to its side, tucked between his legs. He could taste blood in his mouth. The next thing he remembered, Mikey was cradling him in his arms, he was slapping his cheek lightly, "Billy. Billy for Christ sake, it's okay. C'mon I got you." He must have been screaming, or maybe crying, because Mikey kept saying "Shh. Shhh. 'Salright now, bud."

Billy's breathing calmed, and though he could still taste blood, he seemed to be otherwise unharmed. "What happened, kiddo?" Mikey asked, helping his little brother to his feet. But Billy couldn't remember... Then, a series of images struck his head like a baseball bat. He winced and closed his eyes tight...

He was on the ground, looking up, and there was the giant, black gargoyle with glowing red eyes looking down at him from a distance. Then the eyes were closer, seemingly a foot from his own, and they were like fire, burning and dancing, set into a black, hideous face. Then Billy saw his father's face, standing above him, shouting silent curses, spit foaming from his mouth, fury and confusion in his glazed over eyes, fresh beer stains on his shirt. But that image lasted only a second, the next instant it was the red eyes again, but they were farther away now, growing smaller as they ascended into the sky. Smaller, but burning all the same. Billy heard himself scream again, and his brother held him closer, pressing his face into his chest. "'Salright, Bill. Stop that. I got you." Mikey patted his back gently, and Billy quieted again. "Jesus, what the hell happened?"

"I—I got a hit."

"Huh?"

"We won," Billy said. "I wanted to tell you." And a bloody smile appeared on his tear-stained face.

"Yeah. Well, I hope it was worth it. Bike's wrecked." He motioned to the mangled bike at the foot of the tree.

"Oh no. Dad's gonna kill me," Billy said.

Mikey laughed uneasily. "He might actually..." He stopped laughing. "He got fired today."

"Oh."

"Fat bastard's been drunk since noon, asking where the hell you are."

Billy peered over his brother's shoulder, trying to see the black shape on the roof again. But it was gone. The sun was completely set now, and darkness was falling.

Mikey put a hand on Billy's shoulder. "C'mon Bill. Let's get you home." And with a shudder, Billy realized that was the very last place he wanted to go.

1

ARTHUR

ALL THE GOOD LIVING'S DONE...

July 13 ~ Evening

"It's too windy for this shit," Dave said as he dug his shovel into the fresh pile of dirt beside the open grave.

"What'd you say?" Arthur asked, barely audible over the wind's gusty bellows.

"I said it's too damn windy for this!" Dave shouted.

Arthur put down his shovel and walked closer to Dave, his hand tight against his hat as the wind howled against him.

"Say that again, Dave. I can't hear shit in this wind."

"That's what I'm saying," Dave said. "Too damn windy." He coughed and spit phlegm into the grave.

"Too windy to dig a hole?" Arthur asked. "We've done it in worse conditions."

Dave looked around from atop the hill, the few wispy hairs he had left blowing wildly. The cemetery was empty now and growing darker by the minute. "We don't do it at night, goddammit." He spit again.

"Well, we couldn't start piling dirt on the old gal with her family still lurking about now could we?"

Dave grunted. He reached into his pocket and pulled out a pack of cigarettes and a lighter. He put one to his lips and tried to light it. Each flick of the lighter blew out instantly. He spun around, trying to hide his face from the wind. It was no use.

Arthur laughed. "That ain't gonna work out here, genius."

Dave grunted again, then looked down at the brown wooden coffin that lay in the grave, a few scoops of dirt scattered atop the wood. He tapped his temple with his finger, unlit cigarette still in his mouth, then hopped down into the hole and stood on top of the coffin.

He crouched down further to shield himself from the wind and lit his cigarette with ease. "Who's the genius now?" he said from the grave, brown teeth clenched around the white filter.

Arthur laughed again. "That shit'll kill you, ya know?"

"Ha! All the good living has done for me... For us." He tapped the top of the coffin.

"What's that supposed to mean?"

Dave took a long, deep drag, still standing inside the open grave. "Carol took the girls and left me last week," he said. "Well, kicked me out, more like." Dave's voice cracked a bit as he choked back tears.

"Jesus, Dave. I'm... sorry to hear that." In the faint light of the cigarette Arthur could see the burning cherry reflected in Dave's eyes. He looked away. It was nearly nighttime now, the wind still blowing fiercely. "Hey, we better get this done and get out of here. This shit isn't slowing down anytime soon."

Arthur reached his hand down into the grave and pulled Dave out with a grunt. The second Dave was back above ground, the wind stopped. "Thought it wasn't slowing down," Dave said with a smirk.

"I'm no weatherman."

"That's for damn sure." Dave gave Arthur a hard pat on the

back, then motioned toward the open grave. "That family looked kinda rich, wouldn't you say?"

Arthur thought for a moment and shrugged. "I didn't notice."

"Think they buried that old geezer all dolled up?"

"No idea."

Dave looked at Arthur, then down at the coffin, then back at Arthur. "Might be worth a look."

"For the last time," Arthur said, "I'm done with that shit." He looked around the cemetery, still empty. "And so are you. You're not even supposed to be here, remember?"

"Well aren't you just a disciple 'o Christ," Dave chuckled, blew out a puff of smoke, and spit again. "I know I ain't supposed to be diggin' graves no more, but what am I gonna do? Work in a fuckin' coal mine like my old man?" Arthur didn't respond. "Fuck that." Dave spit again.

"Working the mines is no life, we've talked about that. Just be glad I bring you along to help me dig."

"I appreciate ya, Artie. Ya know I do. A man's gotta work somehow. And in this town, you work the mine or you work the shovel. We both know ya can't breathe down in them tunnels."

Arthur thought of the mine tunnels, cramped and dark, and felt his chest get tight. "Let's just finish up and get out of here," he said.

"You're the boss now, Artie" Dave grabbed his shovel then looked over Arthur's shoulder. "Hey, you seein' that?" He motioned toward the town down below the hill and pointed toward something Arthur couldn't see.

"See what?"

"What the fuck is that?" Dave said through the cigarette still in his mouth. "Behind that big gravestone... I swear I saw something."

"Well, what did you see?" Arthur was now standing behind Dave facing the town.

"Some sorta eyes. Like, big red eyes lookin' right at us."

Arthur squinted. "You sure it wasn't just some lights down on Main Street? That's all I see." He turned and grabbed his shovel out of the dirt. "C'mon, let's finish up."

"Jesus Christ there it is, Arthur! Look!"

Arthur turned back toward Dave looking over the hill. And now he saw, two glowing red eyes peering out from behind a large marble gravestone carved in the shape of an angel.

The eyes began to rise above the stone, higher and higher, until both Arthur and Dave's heads were tilted skyward. As they looked on, a sudden lightning strike flashed over the town, and in the flash, Arthur could make out the silhouette of the giant figure, red eyes aglow, with wings spread wide, dwarfing the wings of the stone angel on which the creature stood.

Then the flash of lightning was gone, and darkness fell again. And with the crack of the thunder that followed, Arthur watched the red eyes advance toward him in a blur. He ducked behind Dave, and by the time the thunderous sound was over, the creature was gone. But so was Dave...

The wind picked up just as fiercely as before and Arthur felt something heavy brush against his foot. He looked down at the severed head of his friend, Dave's dead eyes wide in terror, the faint glow of the cigarette still tight in his teeth. The only sound was the howling wind, which almost sounded to Arthur like the flapping of wings, followed by the lingering boom of thunder echoing across the valley.

2

ISN'T THAT RIGHT?

July 14 ~ Early Morning

THE NEXT FOUR hours were a blur.

All Arthur remembered was running... Running flat footed and stone faced... A step-by-step trance that must have led him down the hill, through the cemetery gates, and in the middle of Main Street where he'd apparently been found by a local policeman and brought into the station.

Now there he sat, head hung in a dim lit room, a cheap lamp chained to the ceiling over a wooden table with chairs on either side. A cup of coffee, now cold, sat before him.

"So, tell me again Mr. Novac..." the Sheriff across the table took off his hat and rubbed his forehead as he spoke. "What exactly happened to your friend?"

Arthur kept his head down, speaking softly, "I told you already."

"Right. Well, your friend, uh, Mr. Meyrowitz —"

"David."

"Right. David Meyrowitz. Who was... just keeping you company at work, is that right?" Artur didn't answer. "Mr.

Meyrowitz who has been banned from all cemetery visitation, is that right? The very same Mr. Meyrowitz who used to hold your position as grounds keeper. That is, until—"

"Is that really relevant right now?"

"I'd say so, Mr. Novac. The man has priors. Served two years for gr—"

"I told you what happened."

"He wasn't supposed to be there."

"Well, he was there, then he wasn't. Then I saw—"

"His head," the Sheriff rolled his fingertips on the table.

Arthur nodded. "It fell on my foot." He thought he might be sick right there on the table. The image of Dave's face, rolling across the dirt, that wide eyed stare, the cigarette still burning... Then Arthur remembered the eyes. The red eyes that burned right through him and sent a chill down his spine like a winter wind, even hours later in the confines of a warm, windowless room.

The Sheriff put his fingers together then rubbed his eyes before speaking. "Right. Here's the thing, Mr. Novac. I've had my boys crawling all over that hill for the last 3 hours. There's no sign of anything. No body, no blood even, much less a human head."

Arthur didn't answer. He didn't look up from the table. He just sat there.

"Mr. Novac?"

"I think I want a lawyer."

"A lawyer?" The Sheriff chuckled. "Mr. Novac, you're not being charged for anything. As far as I can see, no crime has been committed."

"Bullshit!" Arthur slammed his hand on the table so hard the plastic coffee cup tipped over and spilled onto his lap. "My friend's been murdered! I saw it happen right in front of me!"

"Calm down, Mr. Novac."

"Well, where is he then, huh? Did he just fly off?" Arthur was looking the Sheriff in the face now, cold coffee slowly dripping onto his legs.

The Sheriff shrugged. "Wouldn't be the first time Mr. Meyrowitz up and vanished, isn't that right?"

Arthur looked away. "That was different," he said softly. "He was... going through some stuff back then."

"Going through some coffins, you mean," he smiled. "See, I know all about your friend already. He disappeared the last time he was under investigation. And now I hear he's been digging graves again."

"I never said that."

"Please, Arthur. You think I'm an idiot? I know you haven't been digging all by yourself. That's brutal work. I still don't understand why you didn't take that job at the new Altchur Mine."

Arthur looked down at the coffee stain on his pants. "I can't work down there," he said quietly.

"Your father worked the mines for years."

"That's what killed him."

"There you go again, Artie... We had this conversation years ago." Arthur could sense the Sheriff's frustration beginning to match his own now. He dropped his head again and watched the coffee slowly drip off the table.

"There's no evidence your father died in that old mine," the Sheriff said gently. "The collapse was minor, structural, a minor *bump*, not a full-blown *rock burst*. That's what all the reports say. Plus, his body was never found."

"So what do you think happened then?"

The Sheriff exhaled loudly. "He probably left, Arthur. You know how hard he took it when your Mom passed."

"Give me a fucking break. We both know people don't leave this town. They're born here, and they die here."

"Mr. Meyrowitz left, isn't that right?"

"I don't believe this," Arthur said under his breath.

"And I don't believe you saw a... a what did you call it again?"

Arthur had almost forgotten the reason he was here... All this pointless talk of the past. "I don't know... It had these eyes. Big red eyes like nothing I've ever seen. And wings like... like an angel, I guess. I don't know."

"An angel?" The Sheriff scratched his head. "Now, Mr. Novac, I told you I didn't suspect you of a crime, but you're flirting with a false statement if I've ever heard one right about now."

"I know what I saw."

Then the door opened and an officer poked his head in. "Sheriff, we got a call about shots fired on Maddison Avenue. Possible homicide."

"Jesus, Lou. It's nearly 5 in the morning." The Sheriff stood up. "This is the most excitement this town's seen all year." He turned and headed toward the door. "Hey Lou, get a towel and wipe up this coffee, will ya? It's gonna stain the table."

"But what about the eyes?" Arthur asked, his voice in a panic.

The Sheriff stopped but didn't turn around to face him. "Go home, Mr. Novac." Then he did turn to face Arthur. "And if you happen to see your friend, do yourself a favor, and tell him I want to talk to him."

"He's dead, you idiot. What don't you understand?"

He chuckled. "Get some sleep, Mr. Novac." And with that, the Sheriff left the room.

3

SOMETHING UNFATHOMABLE...

July 14 ~ Early Morning

BUT SLEEP WAS a stranger that night... Something unfathomable. Every time Arthur closed his eyes, he saw the burning red glow.

He still lived in the house he'd grown up in. Still slept in the same room. But this house hadn't felt like a home since his mother died. It had been a little over six years since then. She'd been diagnosed with cancer about three months before her death, but that wasn't what killed her. Though Arthur's father told him repeatedly (sometimes within his mother's earshot) that a cancer diagnosis was as good as a death sentence. He also said any talk of treatment was just "a big charade" between doctors, patients, and families. Arthur's mother must have thought the same way because she never even let the treatment begin.

It was Arthur who found her...

It was spring. He'd been outside in the front yard, digging in the garden, planting flowers in hopes to bring some vibrance and life to a newly "death sentenced" house. It was the least he could do, after all. His mother always wanted a flower garden. His father, trying to do his part, had bought Arthur's mother a pair of new shoes. They were red, and from what Arthur could tell, rather flimsy. But his father insisted they were in style. His mother called them "Sunday school shoes" and rolled her eyes when she first tried them on. But she had worn them every day since Arthur's father gave them to her.

It had been a dry spring, and digging through the hard dirt in the garden was more difficult than it should have been. The hand trowel Arthur had been using was dull and rusted, so he decided to check the cellar for another one.

As he descended the dark staircase, he could already hear the gentle swinging of the rope. The back and forth rhythmic screeching of the fibers being stretched. He never turned the light on. The glow from the upstairs sunlight that floated down to the depths of the cellar was enough to see it. First, he saw the paint bucket; overturned and empty. Then he saw the shoes; the red straps, rounded toes, and flat heels rocking softly above the bucket, dancing to the tune of the swinging rope.

Though he had not dared to venture into the cellar until months after his mother had been removed, Arthur could sometimes still hear the swinging and swaying and aching of the rope.

And though he could not put his finger on it, ever since then, something began to grow inside Arthur. An itch that he couldn't scratch. A splinter he couldn't see. A bug crawling through his blood that he wished he could cut out and look at. Watch it squirm in his hand as he curled his fingers around it and squeezed.

He and his father never talked about it. When it was mentioned, however briefly, in mourning sessions with the neighbors, his father just called it a "terrible thing." The Terrible Thing.

Arthur had always been told how much he and his mother were alike... From their fascination with old movies to their slim and wiry features. *"You'll end up just like your mother if you keep watching that damn thing all day,"* his father had told him a few times before his mother's death when Arthur sat in front of the black and white television. *"Aww, he's such a momma's boy!"* the older neighbors had said on more than one occasion back then. Perhaps it was his complete rejection of the coal mine that caused folks to create a resemblance to his mother. Because one thing that Arthur was sure of: he was nothing like his father. Even so, Arthur hadn't felt too much like his mother either... that is, until he found her in the cellar that day. Ever since then, the itch that built up in Arthur was without a doubt connected to his mother's death. And he often thought about his own *Terrible Thing*.

Arthur's father died a few months after his mother when the mine he was working in collapsed, though his body was never recovered. This had been difficult for Arthur to accept, and the itch intensified. One Terrible Thing after another... What kind of God would take both parents in the span of a year? *A cruel one*, Arthur thought. Was it possible his father had survived the collapse? And chose instead not to return home to his disappointing son and wifeless house, but to travel the world; a newmade vagabond now free to roam. It wasn't an impossible thing to consider, but it was a depressing one.

His father was a buffoon, but try as he might, Arthur could not dismiss the fact that he had grown closer with him in the short months between his mother's death and his own; like the pressing of brick into mortar, cemented together by their shared grief. The passing of the liquor bottle shared between them in the silence of a motherless house. The only sound was the faint buzzing of the dim light bulb above the kitchen table, and the *smack* and *zapp*ing of bugs flying to their lighted deaths after floating in through open, dusty windows. An unconscious passing of the torch, from alcoholic father to rudderless son. Maybe they weren't so different after all...

Arthur lay in this pit of desperate thought in his bed. His eyes wide open as not to see the burning red ones of the thing that killed Dave just hours earlier in the cemetery. *Don't think about that*, he told himself. It was too much to digest. Arthur had now lost the closest thing he considered to be a friend. Although Arthur was nearly half his age, Dave had taken him under his wing of sorts after his father died. And after Arthur was tasked with burying his own mother, Dave began resuming his former duties as grave digger when no one was around to see. Of course, Dave requested half of Arthur's pay, but as much as Arthur needed the money, he needed the help—and the friendship—a great deal more.

But now he lay alone, thinking of his father and how he might have died, most likely suffocating in the mine tunnels. Perhaps it was better he died that way. The way things were going after Arthur's mother passed, his father was well on his way to drinking himself to death, *drowning in a grave of grain and hops*, Arthur thought.

At least the mine tunnels provided a more admirable death than that. The dirt walls crumbling, Arthur's father watching as the tunnel ceilings fell and the last bit of light was choked out, knowing his breath would be next. Arthur's chest felt tight at the thought. He couldn't breathe. It was as if all the air had been sucked out of the room. Struggling, he finally sat up from his bed and regained his breath, in through the nose, out through the mouth. He waited for a moment for his heart to slow, then stood up and headed for his bedroom door.

Arthur stepped from his room out into the lit hallway. He had left on all the lights in the house, which weren't many. It was a small, modest house. Two bedrooms, one bath. One floor with a tiny cellar for a basement.

Dreary and exhausted, Arthur walked towards the kitchen. Haunting the halls of this house like a stumbling ghost in the night... Much like his father did in the months that followed his mother's death... Except Arthur wasn't drunk. Not yet.

When he entered the kitchen, he went right for the refrigerator. Inside it was nearly as empty as the rest of the house. On the door was an old ketchup bottle and a mug of bacon grease, and on the shelf sat a lonely six pack of beer. That was all. But food was not what Arthur wanted right now. He took a beer from the sleeve and cracked open the can. He stood with the refrigerator door open and drank.

Arthur chugged the first beer quickly, belched loudly, and went for a second. Instead of just taking one beer, he pulled the entire sleeve out and set them on the kitchen table behind him. He turned back to close the refrigerator door and stopped dead...

In the refrigerator, he was staring at the severed head of Dave Meyrowitz.

Dave's head lay on its side, left cheek resting on the shelf where the six pack had been only moments ago. The smoke from Dave's still burning cigarette spiraling upwards toward the ceiling. Arthur could smell the smoke, could feel it choking him.

"Can I get a cold one, Artie?" the head said in a raspy voice.

Arthur continued to stare. He wanted to scream. To run. But he couldn't. He was frozen solid. His feet cemented to the ground.

The head began to cackle... Smoke seeping out of its neck with every exhale...

Then Arthur heard the morning church bell from down the street and looked out the window. Dawn was here already. When the bells stopped, he looked back at the shelf... Empty.

"Jesus Christ," Arthur said to himself. He shut the refrigerator door and walked slowly past the beer cans on the table, out
the front door and into the hazy morning light.

4

DOLORES
THE NEIGHBORS WON'T LIKE THAT...

July 14 ~ Early Morning

DOLORES OPENED her eyes weakly and turned to face her husband in bed. He wasn't there. Not entirely surprising. From what Dolores could tell the sun was just rising, a bright yellow glow on the brink of illuminating her bedroom curtains. She looked at her clock on the bedside table. 6:24 AM. Of course Norman was awake by now. Her husband had never been a great sleeper, something she'd picked up on in the first couple years of their half-century relationship. *Over half a century*, she thought and giggled. 53 years they'd been married. And she could count on both hands the number of times her husband had slept through the morning.

She didn't sleep much herself these days. Old age has a way of taking sleep from you. But Dolores Barnes didn't look at it that way. *She* was the one taking from *life*. And every second she overslept was like leaving a bit of life on the table.

She sat up slowly and let her frail legs dangle over her side of the bed. Her nightgown was bunched up around her knees, and she hated looking at her purple, wrinkled legs. She stood and let the nightgown cover her fully.

She reached for her glasses beside the clock and put them on her face. Her glasses had become thicker and thicker over the last 10 years, and now she thought she looked more like a caricature of an old lady than the once young and fresh girl she'd been. But life had a way of taking things. Sleep, eyesight, beauty, time...

Dolores heard a faint grunting sound from outside and went over to the window. She pulled back the curtain to see her husband pushing the old lawn mower out of the shed in the backyard. *The neighbors won't like that,* she thought. And she couldn't blame them. Who would want to be woken up before 7 AM by their neighbor cutting his grass?

But Norman didn't like the heat. He never had. So, on summer days like this, he'd mow his lawn first thing in the morning, and be finished before the sun could truly start to burn. The sun was rising higher now, shining warmly through the bedroom window. *That was fast,* Dolores thought. *Why does everything have to move so fast?* It wasn't fair. Time was relative. And the older you got, the faster it moved, and the less of it you had. Norman never wanted to talk about these things. She doubted he even thought about them. But she did. And often.

She could smell fresh coffee, so she slipped on her slippers and shuffled slowly into the kitchen. There was half a pot left, so she poured herself a cup and set it on the counter. Then she poured a cup for Norman in a fresh mug to take out to him. Next to the kitchen was a sliding glass door that gave way to the back patio. She stood there for a moment taking in the view.

They lived at the edge of town and had no neighbors behind them, so an unobstructed view of the woods and the field between them was a welcome sight in the daylight, though, at times, a fearful one at night.

Norman was fidgeting with the mower, checking the oil gauge, and brushing last week's dead grass out of the motor's air filter. Dolores took a sip of his coffee and looked over at her vegetable garden at the far end of the backyard. *Maybe I'll cut some asparagus for dinner tonight,* she thought. Gardening was one her few hobbies, and considering she hadn't much of a green thumb, what with the struggling tomato and pepper plants, she thought asparagus was her new favorite vegetable. The stalks grew out of the ground without needing much attention at all. *They don't fuss.* And that's what she loved about them.

It took Norman a few tries to get the mower running. And after a number of tiresome pulls on the string, the old thing backfired loudly and roared to life, blowing a cloud of grey smoke into Norman's face. Dolores watched her husband wave his hands in front of his face, coughing quietly in the smoke. And then she saw the great shadow of some kind of giant bird block out the sun for a moment. It came from the roof, she guessed, and it was advancing on poor Norman. His swinging arms and mild coughing gave way to flailing wild motions and a guttural cry.

Dolores opened the sliding door and stepped onto the back porch. And what she saw over her husband was no bird. No bird at all. It looked like... *No. How could it be?* But it did. It looked like the Nephilim. Something she'd seen illustrations of as a girl back in Hebrew school, before she married Norman and converted to Christianity. She couldn't see the front of it, but its back was adorned with large black wings, and it towered over her husband who had fallen to his knees, one hand on his own chest, wheezing painfully trying to catch his breath.

A strange sensation took hold of her, and Dolores found herself charging at the beast, coffee mug in hand. She felt like a young woman again, running as fast as she could, paying no mind to the painful protests of her old, purple knees. She knocked a rocking chair clean over in her advancement without even realizing it, her eyes dead set on the thing that was attacking her husband.

When she was only a couple feet away, she splashed the steaming hot coffee on the creature's back and then slammed the mug on its spine, shattering the mug and her wrist. But she never felt any pain. She felt only terror when the thing turned its head without turning its body, and she stared into the burning fires of Hell just before life took the very last thing it could from Dolores Barnes.

5

ARTHUR

YOU BARELY TOUCHED YOUR TOAST…

July 14 ~ Midmorning

"MORE COFFEE, HON?"

Arthur looked up from the table he was sitting at. He had ended up at Milo's Diner somehow, in a corner booth at the far end of the restaurant. An empty coffee mug and two pieces of toast with melted butter sat before him on a plate.

"Please," he said, and slid the mug toward the waitress.

"Regular, right? Not decaf?"

"Uh, yeah. Regular. Thanks"

She began to refill his coffee. "You sure you don't want something else to eat, darlin'? You barely touched your toast."

She was a sweet girl. Relatively pretty for a small West Virginia town. Arthur had seen her in the diner before. "I'm really not hungry," he said. "Coffee's good though," Arthur looked up at her as he said this.

Her smile quickly faded, and she jerked her hand just slightly and spilled a bit of coffee. "Oh gosh, I'm sorry! Did I spill on you?"

"No, no. I don't think so," Arthur smiled weakly at her.

She gulped. "Are you alright? You look about white as a ghost."

Arthur looked back down at the table. "I—uh…"

"Looks like you need some sleep, you sure you don't want decaf?"

"I said regular is fine." He pulled the coffee closer to him and pushed the plate of toast toward her. "You can take this, I told you I don't want it."

The waitress gave an uncomfortable kind of half-smile. "Sure thing, hon," she said, took the plate and walked away.

6

MARCUS

SOME KIND OF RUCKUS…

July 15 ~ Early Morning

MARCUS AWOKE to his phone ringing…

He opened his eyes to darkness. The only light came from the digital alarm clock on the bedside table, which read 4:11 am. Marcus could hear the ocean outside his open window; the steady crashing of waves that lulled him to sleep now in a rhythm with the ringing telephone. He wanted to let it go, but after the fourth ring, he answered.

"Hello," he said in a groggy voice.

"Detective," said the chipper voice on the other end. "Good morning. How's vacation?"

Marcus rolled over and found himself slightly tangled in the phone cord. "Relaxing. Sleeping in is just what I needed, Chief."

The voice on the other end chuckled, "Sorry to wake you, Marcus, but something's come up."

Marcus didn't answer. He'd been expecting this. A true, undisturbed vacation was too much to hope for, especially for a man in his position. Marcus Wrathmore was one of the youngest Special Agents the FBI had ever employed. At just 24 years old,

Marcus had investigated and solved over a dozen homicide cases in his hometown of Baltimore. His resume was so impressive, he was plucked from his precinct and graduated from local detective to FBI Special Agent.

The promotion was difficult for Marcus. A man with humble beginnings, he felt he was really making a difference on the streets in Baltimore. For young kids to see a man who looked like them, from the same area they grew up in, single handedly making the city a better, safer place... That was the epitome of a role model in his opinion. But when the Deputy Director of the FBI himself offers you a job, you don't turn it down.

So, here Marcus was, two years into being a Special Agent, finally on his first paid vacation. Sleeping with the window open in a small, musty cottage on the coast of the Outer Banks in North Carolina.

"Detective?" said the voice on the other end.

"I'm here, sir," Marcus replied.

"Well, you're gonna need to be somewhere else, ASAP."

Marcus took a deep breath. Three days into his vacation...

"Where at, sir?"

Marcus's supervisor, acting SAC (Special agent-in-charge), paused for a moment... "Burnwell, West Virginia. Old coal mining town. Appears there's some kind of ruckus being stirred up over there. Quite a few bodies beginning to stack up, I'm told."

Marcus sat up and began to untangle himself from the phone cord. "Are these suspected murders?"

"You'll have to talk to the local department. I'll send you the coordinates."

"How many bodies are we talking?"

"What did I just say? Get down there and talk to them. You want me to do your job for you?"

"No, sir. Sorry, sir. I'll head there right away."

"Good," said the voice, more stern than chipper now. "And Marcus, don't go telling them you're FBI. They don't like Feds down there. Blame us for all kinds of regulations imposed on the mining business."

"What should I tell them?"

"Well goddamn son, tell them you're the fucking tooth fairy for all I care. Just don't tell them you're an agent."

Marcus smiled. It wasn't often his supervisor referred to him as a Special Agent, even though that was his official title. His bosses had the habit of calling him "Detective" as a way to get under his skin. Marcus never bothered to correct them. It was hard enough for a young black man to get the approval of a department that was nearly all white.

The voice on the other end paused for another moment. "Look, just be a good boy and clean this mess up for me. The whole thing has been escalated far enough. Most of the time these idiots can handle themselves, but when I spoke to the Sheriff, he seemed pretty disturbed. Go do your job but do it quietly and calmly."

"Yes sir," said Marcus. And with that, the call was ended, and Marcus threw off the covers and stepped out of the bed. He stood looking out the open window, the white caps of the waves barely visible against the dark blue water and even darker morning sky. *So much for vacation*, he thought. Then Marcus began to pack his things.

7

ARTHUR

BIT OF A SWEET TOOTH...

July 14 ~ Afternoon

"'SCUSE ME." Arthur felt something poking his shoulder and lifted his head up from the table. The sun was high and shining brightly through the window of the diner. He felt a small poke on his shoulder again. "'Scuse me. You were sleeping," said the waitress.

Arthur squinted up at her. "Oh. Sorry," he said. "More coffee, please."

The waitress looked at him. "You been here almost four hours. I refilled your coffee like eight or nine times. Maybe you wanna go home? Get some sleep?" she said timidly.

Arthur rubbed his eyes. "Look, I'll pay for the coffee. Just get me some more."

The waitress looked over her shoulder at the counter behind her. A man wearing glasses and a white button-down shirt with a red tie was glaring at her. He made an aggressive gesture with his thumb toward the door, and Arthur could see him mouth the word "Out" silently.

She turned back toward Arthur. "See, it's just my manager."

She nodded toward the counter. "He says you can't just sit here and not order any food this long."

Arthur sighed. "Fine." He took the half-filled mug of now cold coffee, drank it in one gulp, and stood up to exit the diner. "Coffee here tastes like shit anyway."

As he was walking toward the front door, he passed the display case filled with cakes and pudding cups. On the bottom shelf, between two plates with a slice of red velvet cake on each sat Dave's severed head.

Its eyes looked at Arthur as he passed. "Piece of pie, Artie boy?" Dave said, muffled through the glass.

Arthur stopped. Both the waitress and the manager were staring at him. He looked back at the display case with Dave's head in it. "I'm taking this," Arthur said as he opened the case door, reached down, and grabbed Dave's head by the few wispy hairs on the top.

"Hey! You gotta pay for that!" Yelled the manager from behind the counter.

"Fuck off," Arthur said quietly as he opened the front door and exited the diner.

As he walked down Main Street with Dave's head in his hands, Arthur saw a swarm of policemen surrounding some caution tape on the corner of Maddison Avenue a few blocks ahead.

"Uh oh," Dave's head said. "Looks like a pig pen."

Arthur didn't respond. He spotted the Sheriff speaking to the group of officers and headed straight for him. "Don't be stupid now, Artie," said Dave's head.

"Shut up," said Arthur quietly.

He stood on the other side of the caution tape and called to the Sheriff. The Sheriff looked at Arthur, said something to the policemen, and walked over toward him.

"Mr. Novac. Not getting much sleep, I see." The Sheriff pointed to his own face, touching the skin under his eyes.

"Yeah. Tough to sleep with this thing around." Arthur held up Dave's head to show the Sheriff.

The Sheriff looked puzzled. "Right... Got a bit of a sweet tooth, Mr. Novac?" he asked.

Arthur looked at his hands. He was holding a piece of red velvet cake, cream cheese icing all over his fingers.

"Sugar can keep you awake, Mr. Novac. But if you haven't noticed, I'm dealing with a lot over here." He motioned toward the caution tape. Arthur saw now that the tape was blocking off the front porch entrance of the house on the corner.

Arthur dropped the cake on the ground. "What happened?" he asked.

The Sheriff took a deep breath. "Well... I'm not too sure, to be honest." He looked toward the house. "Seems like there was some kind of shootout here last night."

Arthur could see bullet casings scattered around the side-walk. Then he noticed bullet holes in the upper windows of the house, chunks of siding missing from the roof, and the entire front gutter ripped from the house, now dangling in front of the doorway.

Arthur could hear bits and pieces of muffled conversations between the policemen... "No fucking way these are bullet wounds... Whole family. All of them... Except for the father. All we found was his arm... This ain't right..."

"By the way, Mr. Novac, you might want to finish burying Mrs. Welsh sometime soon. Can't leave her grave open all week, now... Besides," the Sheriff motioned to the crime scene behind him, "gonna be more work for you up at the cemetery here shortly."

Arthur didn't answer, he was busy trying to peer around the Sheriff to get a better look at the scene.

"Any word from your friend Mr. Meyrowitz?" asked the Sheriff.

Arthur rubbed his eyes. "Yeah. He said you're all idiots." He turned away from the Sheriff and walked down the alley that led around to the back of the house. In the backyard, he could see two men in suits talking on the back porch.

"...-already called D.C. They're sending someone."

"Those pompous assholes. They're probably laughing at us."

"We had no choice. Three or four dead here, two others on Culver on the other side of town this morning... All within the hour; sun had barely risen. Shit doesn't add up."

"You can say that again. Never seen anything like this."

The two men saw Arthur and stopped talking. They made their way inside the house to join the officers, and Arthur walked on.

8

TELL YOU WHAT...

July 14 ~ Evening

HE STILL FELT LIKE A ZOMBIE... walking expressionless, one foot in front of the other. No real destination. Like a vehicle that hums along slowly when you take your foot off the gas. Arthur didn't have a vehicle of his own, he couldn't afford one. But he remembered his father teaching him how to drive in the old light blue 1958 Ford F-Series that now sat littered on the front yard of his house like a lawn ornament. Overgrown with weeds and vines that crept their way out of the Earth like arms trying to caress the old truck and pull it under.

The vines could have it, for all he cared. It didn't run anymore. Or maybe it did, Arthur wasn't sure. But there was something wrong with it... Carburetor, fuse block, transmission... One of those words that Arthur never fully understood. Motor vehicles had always been his father's hobby, if a man who worked so much could have a hobby. If he could, Arthur's father would have two: Motor vehicles and drinking; often in conjunction. The latter happened to be a little hobby of Arthur's as well.

At least that was one thing he learned from his father when he was alive.

Alive... Arthur caught himself thinking. *You mean, when he was around?* Arthur heard the Sheriff's voice say inside his head.

Somehow, just like his father used to, Arthur had stumbled his way back to his house, which was just down the road from the diner. It was one of those towns where everything was just down the road from everything else.

He passed by the old truck in the yard, now more of a rust grey than the light blue that used to match the summer sky.

Arthur kicked the front left tire as he walked by and made his way up to the front door. It had been left open, so Arthur walked in and shut the door behind him.

He saw the abandoned beer cans on the little table and reached for one. It was warm. He reached for the refrigerator door handle to put them back inside... But he hesitated.

Perhaps he'd look down in the cellar for a drink instead... His father used to hide bottles of vodka from his mother down there; tucked behind the tool shelf that housed an assortment of hammers, wrenches, saws, and hatchets. His mother must've never bothered looking behind the shelf. She was never thrilled about walking down in the dark, dank cellar to begin with, for all Arthur could remember. Except for that one time... The words "*terrible thing*" played in his head...

Arthur didn't want to go down there, but he didn't want to open the refrigerator either. But he knew his only other alternative was to not drink at all, so...

The door to the cellar creaked when he opened it, and the light from the sunlit first floor dining room pierced through the blackness of the cellar like a beam of yellow, showing only a wooden staircase that descended into more blackness. At the bottom of the steps, faintly visible, was a string that switched on the dim light bulb to the cellar. Arthur almost saw it move. Saw it start to swing gently. But it didn't. It was still and silent.

Each step cried briefly in disagreement as Arthur descended them. He walked slowly, his shadow growing as he crept into the darkness. When he reached the final step, he paused. Looking into the darkness, he placed his hand around the string that hung from the light bulb.

It was quiet. The only sound was a persistent dripping from one pipe or another. Arthur pulled the string, and the room was illuminated in a lazy yellow glow. Cinder block walls crawling with pipes of various sizes that jutted out in all directions like some sort of metallic dystopian calligraphy.

He made his way to the tool shelf and rummaged behind it. The tiny light that hung from the ceiling cast almost no light behind the shelf, but Arthur saw all the familiar appliances sitting there; a handsaw, couple screwdrivers, hammers... all covered in a thick, visible layer of dust, untouched since his father had left. He reached around to the back of the tool shelf, and after feeling his way around for a few seconds, he felt the cool glass of the bottle and picked it up. It was a little less than half full, but it would do the trick.

Before he turned around to walk back up the steps, he could hear it. It was faint, but it was there. The soft, haunting, rhythmic swaying of the rope. He could feel the itch again. He closed his eyes and told himself it wasn't there. And after a few seconds, it wasn't... But something else was. A small thumping sound came from the back corner behind him.

Arthur turned around and saw something move toward him. He felt his heart jump and his stomach drop and he stood frozen. Out of the darkness, Dave's head rolled, just like it had in the dirt beside the grave in the cemetery, end over end into the lazy light of the hanging bulb and stopped upright just below the bottom step.

"Tryna hide from me, Artie?"

It took him a moment to comprehend what the head had said. When he finally did, Arthur responded in a whimper, "What do you want from me?"

The head laughed, and smoke issued from its mouth and out from the floor where its neck touched the ground. There was no cigarette in its mouth this time, but Arthur could smell the smoke all the same.

"Just want a friend, Artie. All this loneliness is going to my head." It laughed again.

"Please," Arthur said, his voice cracked and shaking, "Leave me alone."

The head stopped laughing. "It's your fault, you know," it said. More smoke spilled out of the head's mouth as it spoke, spiraling toward the ceiling in the faint glow of the yellow bulb. "You threw me right in front of it."

Arthur shook his head. He wanted to shout "NO!" but no words would come out.

"Yes," the head said. "Yes, ya goddamn did. And now look at me, no *body* to talk to." The head roared with hoarse laughter.

"Please stop following me," Arthur begged.

"Know what your problem is?" the head said. "You got all this inward rage. What ya need to do is turn that outward. It's the world that's hurt ya, Artie. You gotta hurt it back."

"What do you know about hurt?" Arthur asked.

The head stared at him. "Look at me, what do you think?"

Arthur began to walk back up the stairs. "It'll make the itch stop, guarantee ya that," the head said.

"Maybe I don't want it to stop. Maybe I should just itch it and get it over with." *Such a terrible thing*, Arthur heard in his head.

"Take it from me, bein' dead ain't all its cracked up to be, kid... Tell you what," said the head. "Get me a friend, and I'll prove it. Then I'll leave ya be."

9

JUST A COUPLE SANDWICHES...

July 15 ~ Morning

CONVINCING young Martin Brandt to help him finish burying Mrs. Welsh wasn't the hard part. Martin was as broke as Arthur, so when Arthur said he'd give him a crisp $20 bill for what should only take two grown men an hour or so of labor, Martin was happy to go.

Martin didn't like the mines either, so he was always looking for some kind of supplemental income. From what he told Arthur, his mom wouldn't bug him so much if he just pitched in a little here and there. Martin was 19 years old, a few years younger than Arthur, still living at home on the other side of town. When Arthur came by his house with a couple of shovels over his shoulder and a plastic bag hanging off his wrist, Martin bid goodbye to someone inside the house (his mother, from what Arthur could gather)—*there was the itch again*—and greeted Arthur on the front lawn.

"Artie! Hey man, how are ya?"

Arthur and Martin were familiar, but Arthur wouldn't call them "friends". He usually ran into him at the local bar called

Smitty's. He was a tall, lanky kid with crooked teeth and long, dirty brown hair that fell in front of his face. He pulled his hair back in a ponytail as he approached Arthur.

"Hi Martin," Arthur said. "Ready to get to work?" He handed Martin one of the shovels.

"Sure am!" He took a shovel from Arthur, and they began walking up the street toward the cemetery on the hill, barely visible but fairly close to Martin's house.

When they turned the corner, Martin stopped and pulled out a pack of cigarettes. "Want one?"

"No thanks," said Arthur.

Martin lit his cigarette with a chrome Zippo lighter that reflected the sun into Arthur's eyes, making him squint. "My mom doesn't know I smoke. She says smoking kills you." He smacked the top of the lighter closed and put it back in his pocket.

Arthur shrugged. "All the good living's done us."

Martin gave a wry smile and nodded. They walked in silence for the next few minutes, then entered the cemetery gates and started up the hill.

"What's in the bag?" Martin asked. He took one final drag of his cigarette and flicked the butt.

"Oh." Arthur looked down at the bag on his wrist. "Just a couple sandwiches," he replied.

"Can I have one?"

"Not yet. Let's get to work then eat when we're finished."

They walked up the hill in more silence. It was midmorning now, probably close to noon if Arthur had any guess. As they approached the open grave where Mrs. Welsh had been laid to rest, Arthur passed the large gravestone shaped like an angel. He had almost forgotten about the eyes. The blood red eyes that rose like an ascending giant into the darkness of the night sky. And suddenly, the muffled haze of gloom that Arthur had been walking through rifted, and something else took hold—the bright and shimmering face of terror.

He froze on the spot.

"Artie, you okay?" Martin's muffled voice floated through Arthur's head.

"Yeah," Arthur said quietly. Then he shook his head and turned away from the gravestone. "It's just up here." He pointed to the large pile of dirt beside Mrs. Welsh's open grave.

When they got to the grave, Martin stuck his shovel in the dirt pile and pulled out another cigarette. He cupped his hands around the match but couldn't get it to stay lit long enough to light his smoke. He tried this with two more matches. No luck.

"Try climbing down in there," Arthur said and pointed inside the grave to Mrs. Welsh's brown casket.

"What, just... right on top of her?" Martin looked at the coffin, then back at Arthur.

"Don't think she'll mind much," Arthur motioned him to hop down. Martin did.

While Martin stood in the hole trying to light his match, Arthur looked inside the bag he was carrying. Dave's head was staring up at him. It smiled and winked.

"You can do this, Artie," the head whispered.

Arthur shook his head.

"Yes, ya can. Turn that rage outward. Silence the rope..."

Next to Dave's head was the hand saw Arthur had taken from his father's tool shelf in the cellar. He dropped the bag.

Arthur looked around the cemetery to make sure they were alone. They were. Then he stood over the hole. Martin had just lit his cigarette and was trying to climb his way out of the grave. A few pieces of dirt crumbled from the wall as he struggled upward. When Martin's head finally peaked its way up to the surface, Arthur placed both hands around his shovel and raised it high above his head. Martin lifted his head to look up at

Arthur. He opened his mouth in shock and the cigarette fell to the ground. Then Arthur swung the shovel downward with full force. The way you swing one of those mallets at the carnival, pounding the bell on the ground with all your strength. The blade of the spade struck Martin above his left eye and his body fell into the hole with a thud.

And in that moment, Arthur had to admit there was something freeing about it all... A kind of exhilaration he'd never experienced before. As he lifted the shovel again, a weight was lifted from inside him, and in the rush of the moment, Arthur realized he didn't feel the itch inside his racing blood, nor could he hear the ever-present swinging of the rope.

Martin's body lay face up on the brown coffin, twitching. Blood covered the left side of his face, and Arthur saw a string of flesh hanging from the tip of his shovel. He hopped down into the grave and stood over Martin's body. Martin was breathing heavily, and his limbs moved in sudden, jerking motions, hitting the dirt walls causing more dirt to crumble around him. Arthur took the blade of his shovel and pressed it hard into Martin's throat.

"Your mom was right," Arthur said. "Smoking does kill you."

Using all his weight to push the blade into Martin's skin, Arthur could see more blood start to bubble up out of the gash in Martin's face.

In this moment, Arthur was struck with a memory... He was a youth, maybe 12 or 13. Cutting the lawn in the small yard behind his house with an old push mower. It was a Montgomery Ward Power Mower, and at one time, the nicest, newest mower in the entire neighborhood. His father bought it after seeing a brochure in the mail, and young Arthur was ecstatic when his father finally allowed him to start cutting the lawn himself. He felt like a fancy, rich kid. Mowing the lawn with a motor that spits out fumes like a gas-belching dog that walks itself, while all the other kids had to use manual reel mowers. It was a real responsibility, his father said, and an opportunity to really spruce up the place. Make it stand out in the neighborhood.

Arthur didn't take the responsibility lightly. But after a few weeks of using it, the new mower lost its appeal, and Arthur started cutting the grass with less timid reverence, and more scheduled monotony. It was a mowing session like the latter, on a hot summer afternoon, that this memory took place.

Arthur was walking in that all too familiar, step-by-step zombie trance as the mower hummed along lazily. His mind was wondering off, like a child's mind often does, thinking about Mickey Mantle's batting stance and if the Yankees could win yet another World Series, when the mower suddenly hit what felt like a rock, and the motor starting gurgling and coughing like an emphysema patient. Arthur snapped out of his big-league daydream and shut it off.

He had run over a rabbit. Its frail little body twisted in a knot; the back legs shot out at an unnatural angle where the blade had hit. Its back was completely paralyzed. The back fur was ripped through, showing bloody pink flesh, but the front legs kicked and kicked, spinning itself in a circle in some kind of macabre dance routine. Arthur screamed, and his father came darting out of the house holding a bottle of beer.

Arthur couldn't recall the exact words his father said... Something along the lines of cleaning up your mess and putting the poor thing out of its misery. All in the name of learning a lesson in focus. So, tears running down his face, Arthur took a shovel from the garden and stood over the rabbit. He hit it once or twice weakly with the flat bottom of the shovel head, but the rabbit just kicked harder and continued spinning. His father, red-faced drunk, found this amusing. Laughing, he instructed Arthur to take the blade of the shovel and nestle it tightly between the rabbit's head and neck.

So, Arthur positioned the blade as such. "I'm sorry," he said crying softly. The bunny's eyes were wide and still as Arthur looked down at it... And, following his father's orders, he plunged the blade into the rabbit's neck. It took three stabs before the head was completely removed. And once it was, the front legs still kicked, at one point, even kicking its own head as it spun in a circle.

When it was finished, Arthur wanted to go inside and sleep. But his father insisted he finish what he started and make sure the grass was at an even length. But before he continued his chore, he had to dispose of the rabbit. So, still unsure of why he did this, he used the shovel to scoop up the rabbit's body, no longer twitching or kicking, and tossed it in the backyard to the left of his house. Then, he gathered the tiny rabbit's head and threw it in the neighboring backyard to the right. Perhaps he thought that if he separated the body parts, his crime would be harder to piece together.

These thoughts flashed through Arthur's mind and his eyes glazed over, barely aware of what was happening in the here and now.

Then, in a sensation like the pressure buckling of a bolt into a socket, Arthur felt the shovel collapse Martin's windpipe, and through the handle of the shovel, Arthur could feel the last gasping breaths issue from the skinny boy bleeding out on top of the brown coffin.

Arthur forced the blade of his shovel into the boy's throat until his hands hurt. Then, when he was sure he'd been dead for at least a minute, he tossed the shovel out of the grave and climbed out.

He took the hand saw out of his bag and jumped down into the grave again.

Arthur had never been a good carpenter, and the saw blade was dull and rusted. But after what seemed like an endless back and forth of the blade on Martin's neck, Arthur could tell he was making progress. He tried to pry the head off the body, but it wouldn't come. Then Arthur grabbed the front of Martin's shirt and lifted him up by the chest. The dead boy's head slumped back, still connected by a few tendrils of flesh like a grisly PEZ dispenser.

Arthur dropped the body back onto the lid of the coffin. Suddenly, he was struck with the sudden urge to stop and go to sleep, right there next to boy's dead body inside Mrs. Welsh's grave. But the image of his father insisting he finish what he started crept into his mind. So, after a few familiar whacks with the shovel blade, resulting in the splintering of some wood on the casket lid, Martin's head was sufficiently severed from his body. In a way, Arthur thought his father would be proud.

Tired, hands covered with sweat and blood, Arthur grabbed Martin's head by the ponytail and brought it up to his face.

Only Martin's left eye was intact. The right eye was mashed in the bloody gash that ran from the top of the eyelid to just above the corner of the mouth. Bits of skin hung from the neck like algae clinging to a fishing line that's been pulled from the water.

"Sorry kid," Arthur said. But he didn't cry. He didn't feel much of anything other than the terror of the red eyes that still appeared whenever Arthur closed his own.

Arthur placed Martin's head on the ground above and was about to climb his way out of the grave, but then he stopped. Crouching down on top of the coffin, he rummaged inside Martin's pocket until he found the Zippo lighter. He held it up to his eye to see his reflection in the chrome; blood spattered across his cheek, dirt caked and crusted into the lines of his face. Then he put the lighter in his left pocket and tossed the bloody hand saw and shovel down on top of Martin's headless body.

"Trade ya," he said quietly. Then he scrambled out of the grave and placed Martin's head in the bag next to Dave's.

"Jesus, Artie," Dave's head said. "Coulda found me a prettier friend than this."

Artie looked at both heads sitting face up in the bag. The creature that decapitated Dave had certainly done a cleaner job in the execution.

"He's only got one eye, for Chrissake," Dave's head gave a retching sound.

Artie tied the bag shut, grabbed the shovel Martin had stuck in the pile of dirt above, and began shoveling dirt into the grave, finally finishing the burial of old Mrs. Welsh.

10

MARCUS

BETTER WEEKS…

July 15 ~ Midday

THE DRIVE WAS long and uneventful. Marcus made it from the sands of Rodanthe, North Carolina to the hills of Burnwell, West Virginia in just over eight hours. He reckoned he could have gotten there sooner had he not stopped for lunch in Raleigh.

The surroundings had gotten increasingly more desolate the further into West Virginia he drove, and by the time he stopped for gas in a little town called Ghent, about 40 miles outside his destination, Marcus could sense the hostility growing with each unwelcomed glance he received.

Seeing a black man wearing a suit and tie was probably about as common as seeing a ghost to these people, Marcus thought. And he could guess which sighting they might think scarier. But he would pump his gas, smile and wave, and continue on his way. He was blessed, after all. Not even in his wildest daydreams as a child could Marcus have imagined he'd be sent on "secret missions" to solve cases for the government. And though his superiors may have given him the least desirable assignment they could; he was determined not to let them down. Would the locals make his job easy? Doubtful. But Marcus was used to adversity. Besides, in the words of his late father, "no matter where you go in the world, people are just people". Life was easier when he remembered this.

The highway crested over a hill that looked out over the small town of Burnwell. The road had been cut out through the top of the mountain, so the rock sediment was visible on either side of the highway at the peak. Marcus thought about the millions of years of pressure that caused the formation of the rocks to appear the way they did; different rock types stacked beneath the Earth's crust like a layered cake. He was getting hungry again.

Burnwell Exit 26A, the street sign read, and Marcus followed the exit down a winding road that led to the town. He drove slowly as he approached. The town was much smaller than anything he was used to. There wasn't even a population or welcome sign to greet travelers from what Marcus could see.

The sun was bright and brilliant, and he could see the golden glow coming from the top of a nearby hill and noticed the silhouettes of gravestones adorned there. He could see no obvious evidence of a coal mine, though he realized he probably wouldn't recognize a mine entrance if he did happen to see one.

He could, however, recognize a restaurant sign when he saw one, and the one he drove by read: *Milo's Diner: Breakfast, Lunch, and Dinner!* His stomach rumbled as he passed it. He wanted to stop for a bite to eat, but he knew to check in at the police department first so they could phone his supervisor that he'd arrived without too much of a delay.

Being such a small town, the police department wasn't difficult to find. And when he found it, Marcus parked his unmarked car next to a row of squad cars in the parking lot and went inside.

He opened the front double glass doors to an empty lobby. A

young, uniformed officer sat behind the counter writing something in a notepad. Marcus walked up to the counter and cleared
his throat.

"Excuse me," he said. "I'm looking for Sheriff Renfield."

The officer didn't look up, just put up a finger on his
nonwriting hand, signaling *in a minute*. Marcus stood patiently.
He could hear faint voices coming from the hallway toward the
back of the building but couldn't make out any discernible
words.

"Alright," the officer said, still writing with his head down,
"just a sec." He finished writing and made an aggressive punctu-
ation mark with his pencil. "What can I help—" he looked up at
Marcus from across the counter. "What's going on?" he asked.

Marcus smiled. "I'm looking for the Sheriff," he said calmly.

"What for?" The officer wrinkled his brow.

"Uh, well..." Marcus laughed. He knew there would be push-
back, but this soon? "He should be expecting me."

The officer studied him for a moment, then stood up from
his chair and looked toward the hallway. "One moment," he
said, then walked toward the hallway, looking back frequently to
keep an eye on Marcus.

He knocked on one of the doors in the hallway, the faint
voices stopped, and the door opened from the inside. The officer
who was at the desk said something quietly, then another
uniformed officer poked his head out the doorway and looked at
Marcus. Then his head disappeared into the room and
numerous other officers poked their heads out like prairie dogs
out of the dirt.

Then an officer with a cowboy hat emerged from the room
and walked toward Marcus.

"Eric Renfield," the man said and stuck out his hand.

"Age—er, Detective Wrathmore. Marcus. How do you do?"
The two men shook hands and looked one another in the eye.

"Well, to be honest," the Sheriff said, "I've had better weeks." He looked over his shoulder back down the hallway. Four or five uniformed officers stood in the hallway now looking at Marcus. Some with their arms folded, some with their hands on their hips. The desk clerk walked sheepishly back to his chair behind the counter.

"Philly," the Sheriff said to the young officer behind the counter, "did you offer the Detective something to drink? Water? Coffee?" he said looking back at Marcus.

"No, thanks," Marcus said. "I could use a hot meal, though, to tell the truth."

"Alright then," the Sheriff clapped Marcus on the back. "Let's go grab a bite. You can ride with me. I'll give you the rundown on the way." The Sheriff put his hand out toward the door and motioned Marcus to go first.

As he exited the building, Marcus looked back and saw the group of officers walking into the lobby, watching through the glass double doors as he and the Sheriff made their way to the Sheriff's truck.

11

ARTIE

STREETLIGHTS...

July 15 ~ Midday

THE STREETLIGHTS WERE DIM, and they extended on each side of
the street in parallel lines that stretched forward like train tracks
into the night.

It was night... or dusk... or maybe dawn. It was hard to tell.
But the sky was dark and colorless. The kind of darkness that
you could mistake for a black ceiling. Almost like a blanket that
shrouded everything Artie could see.

Except for the streetlights.

So, Artie walked forward, step by step down the middle of
the road. There were no cars, no people, no sign of life at all.
Streetlamps floated by him as he walked, and Artie noticed
the ground was wet. The kind of wet that sticks to the road
after a light rain. There were no discernable puddles, but
Artie could hear a faint dripping sound that echoed
throughout the street like a leaky drainpipe in a damp
basement.

He walked on and passed more light posts, but there was no
end to them. 20, 30, maybe more he passed by, and still the street

stretched on. As he walked, the dripping sound became a little louder with each pair of streetlamps he passed.

Then he noticed what he was walking toward. It sat there in the middle of the street, a sort of cylindrical rock formation of stones stacked on top of each other. And as Artie got closer, he realized it was a well. The stone walls on the outside were maybe three or four feet high, and the dripping sounds were much louder now and echoed out from the open mouth of the well. As he approached it, he noticed something moving on the backside, just barely visible over the stones.

Moving closer, he saw it was a little girl, dancing arrhythmically to no music Artie could hear. She had dirty, knotty, blonde hair, and wore a stained nightgown that clung to her skin like wet cloth on a clothesline. In her left hand she held a doll in brown clothing, and every few moments would flail the doll out as if it was dancing with her.

Artie watched her from the other side of the well. But when she saw him, she stopped dancing. She dropped the doll and stared at Artie; her head tilted like a dog begging for scraps at the table. The dripping sound from the well was even louder now. The two of them locked eyes for an indiscernible and uncomfortable amount of time, then the doll's soft slumped body jumped up on one of the stones atop the well and began dancing in the same jerking movements as the girl had been.

The girl still stared, tilted head, at Artie. Then Artie noticed the doll didn't have a head, just arms and legs moving in random twitches. And it struck Artie that this wasn't a dance, it was the involuntary movement caused by a cadaveric spasm, much like Martin's postmortem in the open grave.

And with this revelation, Artie looked back at the girl, who now had a sinister smile that was much too wide for her face. He watched as a centipede crawled across her teeth, out of her mouth, and scurried along behind her head.

Artie took a step backward and the girl began to laugh. A laugh that turned to a high-pitched wail that echoed out of the well. The girl's mouth was still too wide, and her eyes were screaming too. The kind of thing a child's eyes will do when they cannot express anymore pain through crying. Her eyes screamed to Artie for help, begging him to make it stop. But he couldn't. So, all of it persisted; the wailing, the contortion of the doll, and the dripping of the well.

All of these were peaking to a crescendo, and then a clawing sound screeched out even louder. Something was scratching its way up from the darkness of the well. The girl stopped screaming and her mouth shut closed, but her eyes were still locked on Artie's, and they screamed silently. The clawing on the stone became clearer and harsher, and before Artie could move, or even look away from the girl, the creature emerged from the darkness of the well. Its red eyes fixed on the girl as it rose out from the darkness and towered over her, though half its body remained beneath the ground. The girl never looked away from Artie. Then the creature's long black claws ripped through the girl's gown and pulled her down into the darkness, and Artie woke up.

12

MEN ARE ALL THE SAME...

July 15 ~ Afternoon

HE AWOKE with his boots on; dried mud now caked onto the sheets at the foot of the bed. He was still fully clothed, dirt and blood stains on his tattered jeans and flannel shirt. His bedroom light was on, and the dusty ceiling fan spun lazily over him, casting a revolving shadow over his face every few seconds.

He could still see the eyes from his dream; the girl's and the creature's. Both equally disturbing.

For a moment he couldn't recall the girl's face. Then it came to him... First the eyes, the screaming eyes. Then the mouth, the widening smile, the insect across the teeth. Then the hair... He had seen her before, and now he remembered where. She was Dave Meyrowitz's youngest daughter.

And in that moment, Artie realized he must do what he'd been dreading since the day Dave died... He was going to see Carol Meyrowitz.

The Meyrowitz's lived at the edge of town in a neighborhood not much different than Artie's. Most of the houses were one story ranchers, some with a one car garage attached to them.

The Meyrowitz's didn't have a garage, but they did have a corner lot at the far side of the neighborhood.

When he arrived, Artie walked through the front yard which was plain but well-manicured. Before he approached the porch that led to the front door, he walked around the side of the house and peered over the fence that surrounded the Meyrowitz's backyard. The backyard looked out at an expanse of deep, dark, deciduous forest, with a clearing off to the far right. In that clearing lay nestled the entrance to the abandoned Dribble Creek Colliery, the very same mine that Artie's father worked in years ago. It sat there innocently yet carried tremendous gravity; like a black hole surrounded by a swirling, living galaxy.

Artie looked at the mine entrance and shivered at the thought of the descending blackness that sat beneath the nearby ground. For a moment, he thought he heard a faint, soft crying in the distance. Almost like a child, though perhaps a young fox. Then he heard an owl hoot loudly in the forest to his left and walked quickly back to the Meyrowitz's front door.

It took him a few minutes to build up the courage to knock. But he did it. Three weak taps of his knuckles on the wooden door. He stood there waiting for another minute or so. Maybe Carol wasn't home. Maybe she was and just didn't want to see him. Something was telling him to forget about it and walk away. But instead of leaving, he gave one more knock, a full knock with his fist. Seconds later, the door opened.

It was the little girl Artie had seen in his dream. She stood in the doorway wearing a blouse, this time clean, with her messy blonde hair in unbrushed knots; the kind of bedhead that Artie himself was sporting. She looked him up and down but didn't say a word. Artie didn't say anything either. They both stared at each other. Her face was roughly the same as it had been in Artie's dream, though her eyes weren't screaming and her mouth was proportionate. She still had a slight look of terror in her eyes; it was faint, but it was there. Perhaps she'd had a nightmare as well, Artie thought. Maybe they were both haunted.

Artie heard a voice come from inside the house. "Well, who is it, Dani?" The girl didn't answer, only continued to stare at Artie. "Danielle Marie, who is at the door?" the voice called again. Then Carol appeared behind her daughter and opened the door all the way.

"Arthur," Carol sounded surprised. "I been tryin' to call you for days now." Artie smiled weakly and shrugged. "Dani, next time answer me when I ask you something." Carol guided her daughter out of the way and motioned Artie inside. "And don't leave guests waitin' on the porch. It's rude." She smiled at Artie. "Come on in Arthur, have a seat."

Artie walked into the house. He had been here a few times before to watch Steelers games with Dave. It was messier than he remembered. There were toys and clothes scattered across the living room floor and dirty mugs and plates on dinner trays next to the sofa.

Carol picked up an ashtray on the seat of the couch and brushed some ashes on to the floor. "Sit down Arthur. I'm sorry this place is such a mess." She looked around the room and smiled nervously. "Girl, I told you to clean this mess up."

The little girl started picking up the scattered toys and making a pile of them in the corner.

"Would you like somethin' to drink, dear? Water, coffee?"

"Coffee, sure," Artie said.

Carol disappeared into the kitchen for a moment, then called out from behind the wall. "I'll have to put a pot on. Just a few minutes."

"Oh. It's okay then. Water is fine," Artie said. He was watching the girl put her toys in a pile and noticed a doll on the floor beside her. It was wearing a polka dot dress and still had its head intact.

"Oh hush, it'll only be a few minutes," Carol said as she rounded the corner holding a glass of water and came back into the living room. "Plus, I already put it on." She handed the glass of water to Artie.

"Oh, thanks," he said as he took the glass. He took a small sip and looked at his feet.

"So, I tried callin' your house," Carol said, putting a cigarette to her lips. She offered one to Artie, and he shook his head. She took the ashtray and placed it on her knee, then lit her cigarette and blew smoke out above her head.

"Yeah, um, I think the phone is broke." The phone wasn't broken. Artie had heard it ring a few times in the last couple days but never bothered to answer. In the middle of the night, he took it off the hook. He could picture it dangling by the cord against the wall as he sipped his water. He wasn't much of a talker anyway.

"Well," Carol went on. "The Sheriff came by the other day and told me Dave was workin' with you at the cemetery..." She paused, looking at Artie for some kind of response. He gave none. "He's not supposed to be doin' that work no more, ya know." Artie continued to stare at the floor. "Anyway, the Sheriff said you seemed kina spooked when he spoke to you the other day. And he was askin' if I seen Dave, which, o'course, I hadn't... We split up, ya know."

Artie nodded.

Carol let out a sigh thick with cigarette smoke. "Look," she said. "I just hate to see you get mixed up with all that again. Dave's no good, ya know."

"Dave's dead," Artie said quietly, still looking at the ground.

Carol reached out her hand and touched Artie's knee. "Listen—"

"He's dead, Carol. I saw it." Now Artie looked at her. She didn't look upset, more concerned.

She looked over her shoulder. "Sweetie, go brush your teeth," she told her daughter. The little girl stopped cleaning up her toys and walked quietly out of sight. "Arthur," Carol said softly, "the Sheriff told me 'bout what you said... Dave's a manipulative son of a bitch. Trust me, I know. So, whatever happened out there, just know you can tell me where he went. I won't tell nobody." She patted Artie's knee.

"I did tell you. Something killed him. Something with glowing red eyes. I saw it."

When he said this, Carol took her hand off his knee quickly and looked behind her shoulder again towards where her daughter went. She looked back at Artie and wrinkled her brow. "What do you mean?"

"This... thing. It had huge red eyes, and it was fast. And it came at us. At Dave. And it... it killed him." He looked back at the floor. "Took his head clean off," he whispered.

Carol put her hand on her chest. She sat for a moment looking puzzled. Then her eyes lit up and she put her hand to her mouth. "Dani... Dani said somethin' like that," she said quietly through her hand. "Said she saw somethin' out her window. Some kinda red eyes or somethin'." Then Carol's face turned to anger. "That son-of-a-bitch is stalkin' us. Tryna scare me. Thinkin' I'll come crawlin' back to him at the first sign of a spook, goddamn him." She took a deep inhale of her cigarette, the white paper rapidly turning to grey ash that crept toward her mouth.

"It wasn't him, Carol. I told you; he's gone. I saw it myself."

She let out a cloud of smoke.

"And," Artie said quietly. "I had a dream that you girls might be in trouble."

Carol's eyes went like sharp little slits. "And what? You

thought you'd be my knight in shinin' armor?" She laughed and shook her head. "King Arthur come to save the day!"

"I just thought—"

"Just stop," Carol said. She scratched her cigarette out on the ashtray on her knee. "You men are all the same."

Artie didn't say anything. He sat there looking defeated, feeling embarrassed, wondering why he even bothered coming here.

"Where's his body then, Arthur? How come they ain't found nothin'? No sign of him." Her voice was getting louder, but still in a controlled sort of anger.

Artie shook his head. "I don't know..." He looked at the ground again and took a sip of water, his hand shaking and spilling a few drops onto his pants. "I've been, like, seeing his head though." He looked back up at Carol. "It's been following me."

"The hell are you talkin' about?"

"His head. I've been seeing his fucking head everywhere I go. He won't leave me alone."

Carol looked at him. She was pretty when she was concerned. Gentle, Artie thought. He felt silly even talking like this to her.

"Have you been drinkin', Arthur?"

He shook his head.

"When's the last time you slept?"

"I'm not crazy," Artie said softly. "I know what I saw."

Carol stood up and took the glass of water from Artie. "Look, you're scarin' me, and Dani's been spooked enough as it is—"

The front door opened and another girl, this one taller, chubby with long light brown hair walked into the room.

"And where the hell have you been?" Carol said sternly to the girl.

This was Carol and Dave's older daughter, Artie remembered, but he hardly recognized her. She had grown quite a lot over the last year or so, he thought. She looked like her mother in the face, albeit more rounded, and like her father with her broad belly.

"I told you I was staying at Jenny's house last night." The girl looked at Artie and he waved sheepishly. She didn't acknowledge him.

"Oh really? Because I called Jenny's mother, and she said you two weren't there." Carol folded her arms across her chest and leaned on one hip.

"Jesus Christ, mom, we went to a party."

"Excuse you? Don't use that kind of language with me." She motioned toward Artie, "Especially in front of a guest."

"Right," the girl rolled her eyes. "So sorry." She walked through the room and into the kitchen, leaving black stains from her shoes on the carpet.

Carol saw this and yelled, "And take off your filthy shoes, Theo! You're getting' mud all over my house!" Carol went to the closet in the hall and pulled out a vacuum. "So sorry for this," she said to Artie. "Teenagers."

Artie shrugged.

Carol turned on the vacuum and started to clean. The vacuum gave a rocky, sediment kind of sound as it went over the footprints. Carol turned it off and bent down to inspect the carpet. "Theo, what is this?" she said.

The girl poked her head out of the kitchen. "Mud. I don't know. Sorry."

Carol touched the carpet with her hand then rubbed the black leavings between her fingers and sniffed them.

"This isn't mud, missy. It looks like soot."

13

KIDS, YA KNOW?

CAROL STOOD UP. "Don't tell me you've been hangin' round that old mine again. Is that where y'all were?"

"For Christsake, mom, we were just with some friends. It's fine."

Carol said nothing, just folded her arms and stared.

"We didn't go in!" The girl insisted.

Carol shook her head. "How many times have I told you?" She threw her arms in the air. "You know what, you can clean this mess up and then go straight to your room. I don't wanna see you til dinner is ready."

"Oh my God," the girl said and rolled her eyes. "Dad was right, you're fucking crazy." She disappeared into the back of the house.

Carol stood with her mouth open but she didn't say anything, she just watched her daughter storm out of the room and then she burst into tears.

"Oh God," she sobbed. "I'm sorry about that, Arthur."

Artie stood up from the couch and walked over to her. He stood behind her as she cried, not knowing exactly what to do.

Comforting a crying woman had never been Artie's strong suit, though, to be fair, he hadn't had much practice.

"Hey," he said, giving a halfhearted, quiet laugh and putting one hand on her shoulder. "Kids, ya know?"

Carol turned toward him and put her face in his chest. "I'm sorry," she cried. "It's just been nothin' but fights with her since her father left." Her tears started to leave wet stains on the front of Artie's shirt.

He went to put his arms around her but stopped midway. Instead, he patted her back as she continued to cry. He could smell her hair now, it smelled sweet. Like flowers and candy. He closed his eyes and took a deep breath, inhaling all her scent and letting it tickle his brain.

"Psst, Artie…" He heard a raspy whisper and opened his eyes to see Dave's head sitting on the living room coffee table smiling at him.

Artie let go of Carol and told her he had to leave, stumbling as he walked and fumbling at the door handle as he opened it. She wiped her eyes with the back of her hand and bid him farewell with a wave.

He walked briskly down the street away from the house as fast as he could without running. All the while, Dave's head floated behind him like a child carrying a forgotten and unwanted balloon on his wrist. A block down the street, the head caught up to him. "You should fuck her, Artie," it said.

"I thought you were gonna leave me alone now," Artie said through a closed mouth. He wasn't sure if anyone might be watching him through their windows; fingers peeling back curtains and peeking through blinds, snickering about what a poor, crazy fool Arthur Novac had become.

"And what? Hang out with that one eyed hippie you brought me? Not a chance."

Artie put his hands to his face and rubbed his eyes. "You should fuck her," the head said again. "Really, I won't mind."

Artie walked briskly the rest of the way home, not engaging with the head that floated along beside him. When he finally arrived at his house, he opened the front door just enough for his slender frame to squeeze inside, then shut it quickly, leaving Dave's head floating in the front yard.

He locked the bolt on the door then leaned his back against it and took a deep breath. He could smell the dampness of the basement and realized he must've left the cellar door open. As he walked over to the cellar steps to shut the door, he thought of Carol. The way she smelled. The flowers and candy. He closed his eyes and tried to smell her again. Thinking about her head resting against his chest; her crying breaths matching the subtle fluttering of his heart, beating merely inches away, just a thin layer of flesh and bone separating them.

Maybe he should comfort her in the way Dave suggested. He'd always found her attractive. Not that there was much competition in a dirty West Virginia mining town like Burnwell. Plus, he'd practically been given the greenlight from Dave himself. What was left of him, anyway. Dave never respected his marriage much when he was alive, from what Artie could tell. He'd seen him flirt and get handsy with anything that moved and had breasts. And on more than one occasion Artie had vowed an oath of silence when Dave left the bar with one piece or another and took them into his beat-up Chevy Bel Air. Most of the time Dave would then stumble back into the bar 10 or 15 minutes later with a shit eating grin on his red face, order another beer and light up a smoke, picking up wherever the conversation had left off.

Dave was far from what Artie would consider an attractive man, but he supposed the women Dave would go after didn't have very high standards to begin with. But somehow, he ended up with Carol...

Though getting your high school sweetheart pregnant at 17 was one way to make them stay, Artie figured. But he'd never had much luck himself when it came to women. Never had much interest, really. There had been a few dates here and there over the years, but after climax was reached, Artie found it extremely difficult to find the woman he'd been with the least bit interesting. But it wasn't for lack of trying. He knew how shallow and downright shitty it was to feel such a way after the deed was done, but he couldn't figure out why it happened to him like that. He figured there was just something wrong with him; he couldn't love. Not after sex. So, to spare the hearts of bachelorettes throughout the town, Artie hadn't dated much. But Carol...

Artie went to the refrigerator and pulled out a beer. But before he cracked the can open, he decided he'd rather have a glass of ice water instead. He put the can of beer back and grabbed a dusty glass from the cabinet. He blew the dust off the glass and opened the freezer for some ice cubes. When he opened the freezer door, he saw the frozen head of Martin, his mouth agape and his bludgeoned eye hanging from a single tendril of flesh. Ice crystals had formed around his one good eye and mouth, and the gash down his face was a frozen reddish brown. Startled, Artie jumped back and dropped the glass, and it shattered across the floor.

He slammed the freezer door shut.

"Told you he was ugly," he heard Dave's raspy voice say. The head was sitting on the pantry shelf to the left of the fridge. Artie jumped again and yelled "fuck!"

"Howddaya think I feel?" Dave's head said. "I ain't lookin' at that fella no more. You butchered it, Artie."

Artie put his hands over his eyes for a moment, then pulled a beer out of the fridge and cracked it open.

"How about gettin' me something prettier to look at?"

Artie took a long drink, then looked at Dave's head. "Fuck off."

"Now now, Artie. Don't be like that. You promised to help me, remember?"

"I don't remember that at all actually." Artie took another drink.

"Don't make me remind you that this is all your fault," the head said. "Just get me a little girlfriend and do it neat this time."

Artie shook his head and took another, longer gulp of beer.

"Plus," added the head, "it helped with your itch last time, didn't it?"

Artie took another drink.

"Ain't hearin' that rope swing much either is you?"

And another drink.

"I know killin's a terrible thing, Artie. But... it ain't unforgivable. There's only *one* unforgivable sin..." Dave began mimicking the sound of a rope swinging. "*Erree, erroo, erree, erroo.*"

Artie put his hand on his forehead and closed his eyes. "Who'd you have in mind?"

The head made a thinking face for a moment, then said, "how about that little minx from the diner? Always wanted a taste o' that."

Artie took another drink, this time finishing the beer. He crumpled the can, then reached for another.

14

MARCUS

GANG VIOLENCE...

July 15 ~ Afternoon

THE SHERIFF TURNED LEFT out of the police lot and pulled out a pack of cigarettes. He put one to his lips, then offered one to Marcus.

"No, thanks," Marcus said from the passenger seat with a small wave of his hand.

The Sheriff shrugged, lit his smoke, then rolled down the driver's side window an inch or two. "You don't mind, do you?" he asked Marcus.

Marcus shrugged. "It's your truck." He used the crank to roll down the passenger side window. He rolled it all the way down, and he could feel the cool breeze of a summer evening rolling in.

"You ever been to West Virginia before?"

Marcus shook his head. "No sir. Never been West of Richmond until this morning."

The Sheriff nodded. "Good folk out here. Quiet." He tried to ash his cigarette out the window, but Marcus saw the ashes fly back into the truck and land on the Sheriff's lap. "They're not accustomed to seeing stuff like what's been going on the last few days."

Marcus looked out the window as the Sheriff drove. Not much activity on a summer evening. They passed three blocks of houses but didn't see a soul in the neighborhood. No one was walking outside or playing in the yard or sitting on the porch, and only a few houses even had lights on inside. "Such as?"

The Sheriff took a long drag from his cigarette, then exhaled loudly. "You ever see much gang violence up there on the streets?"

"Sure. All the time," Marcus said.

"Do the shooters ever... er, mess with the bodies afterwards?"

"What do you mean?"

"Mutilate the bodies. After the shooting." The Sheriff ashed his cigarette again with his left hand and placed his right wrist casually over the steering wheel.

"Not usually, no. Most gang violence is centralized in certain areas. And it's mostly a numbers game to them. 'How many of your guys can we take out and how fast'... That sort of thing."

The Sheriff nodded his head again but didn't speak. He didn't look at Marcus, just kept smoking and looking out his window to the left every few seconds. They drove slowly.

"Well," Marcus added. "There was one guy, part of a newly formed gang in Southwest Baltimore, that used to carve the gang's symbol into the flesh of his rival victims. Apparently, he acted alone in this, and just did it to send a message. Territorial or otherwise. And this was an isolated incident. Just a lunatic trying to make a name for himself."

The Sheriff nodded, and they sat for a minute in silence. "Sheriff," Marcus said. "You think we could grab that bite to eat now? I sure am hungry." He touched his stomach, and it began to rumble quietly. "Long drive and all."

"In a minute," the Sheriff replied. "There's something I wanna show you first. While we still got some daylight."

The Sheriff took a right down another street that was lined with houses on either side. Modest homes, most of them neatly kept. At the far-left corner of the block they were approaching, Marcus could see the ropes of caution tape that extended out to the front lawn of the corner house. The Sheriff pulled up in front of the house and parked his truck.

"Walk with me," the Sheriff said, and both men exited the vehicle. The Sheriff took one final drag of his cigarette, then tossed the butt into the bed of his truck. He led Marcus under the caution tape, and they stood on the walkway that led to the front porch. "About 6am yesterday morning, neighbors all up and down this street reported a heap of gunfire. Some said 10 shots, others 50. From the casings we found," the Sheriff bent down and picked up a shotgun shell casing that was in the grass beside the walkway, "and supposedly cleaned up..." He handed the casing to Marcus. "We guess it was somewhere between 15-25 shots fired."

Marcus examined the casing closely. "All 12-guage rounds?"

"No, actually. We found a few 20-gauge and even some 9mm casings."

"Bodies?" Marcus asked.

"Four, well... three really. Mom and two kids. We think we found the father's—um—well, we found just his arm."

"His arm?"

"George Callaway. Big guy. Good miner. Bit of a drinker. Had a few domestic calls to the house over the years, but nothing that would've resulted in this."

"Resulting in his wife blasting his arm off, you mean?"

The Sheriff winced. "I'm not convinced that's what happened."

"What about the bullet wounds?" Marcus asked. "Any indication of which bullet struck who?"

"Well, you see... None of them appeared to be shot. Their bodies were found mangled and beaten. Ripped apart in some places. Except for the dad, of course." The Sheriff took the casing back from Marcus and put it in his pocket. "In fact, we believe the victims to be the shooters."

Marcus stepped in front of the Sheriff and walked up to the porch. "So, Mom with the 9, one of the kids with the 20, and they blow Daddy's arm off and he runs away?"

The Sheriff shrugged. "Look, we have no idea where Big George is, but his arm wasn't 'shot off'. It looked more torn from his body. Tendrils spilling out at the shoulder." The Sheriff bowed his head and blessed himself. "As for the shooters, probably Dad, Mom, and the older boy. The younger boy, Billy, just turned 12 last week." He blessed himself again.

Marcus inspected the side of the house, noticed the bullet holes in the wall near the front door and the shattered window on the first floor. He stepped off the porch back onto the front lawn and followed the trail of bullet holes up to the second story. More shattered windows and roof shingles torn and missing, the front gutter hung down toward the front lawn like a tiny slide.

"What the hell were they shooting at?"

"That, Detective, is the question."

15

ARTIE

YOU SURE ARE UGLY...

July 15 ~ Evening

DECAPITATING the waitress was the easy part; she didn't put up much of a fight. Artie waited for her shift to end. And once it did, she exited the diner, lit up a cigarette, and turned down into the dark alley beside the diner and began her walk home. Artie approached quietly, asked her if he could bum a smoke, and cornered her as she reached inside her purse to retrieve one. A brief struggle ensued that left Artie with no more than a few scratches on his arms and face. Her nails did some damage as he strangled her, but nothing a few drinks couldn't fix.

The hard part was the waiting...

The hours Artie spent leaning against the wall of the pharmacy that sat across the street from the diner...

The numerous times the pharmacy cashier came outside to politely remind Artie that loitering was illegal...

The number of scowls he received from patrons walking out of the establishment; some carrying paper bags of prescriptions, others unwrapping the cellophane on their cigarette packs and lighting up a smoke as soon as they walked out the door.

And the hardest part: the wrestling that went on in Artie's sleep deprived and tortured mind as he waited. He liked this girl (so did Dave). He wished her no ill will (unlike Dave). And never before had he laid his hands on a woman in violence (probably unlike Dave).

But violence is, without a doubt, what occurred. Artie left the body of the poor girl in the alley. The new hand saw he had bought from the hardware store earlier that day he threw in the dumpster behind the diner. It was much easier to use a fresh, sharp blade as opposed to the dull one he'd used on Martin. And Dave's severed head agreed. Dave's head had cheered Artie on as he worked the saw on the waitress, giving encouragement such as, "Look at you go, Artie!" and "God, I can't wait to put my tongue in there!" Artie did his best to ignore him, but the sounds of pleasure Dave's head made as Artie cut off the waitress's were so lewd and campy, Artie couldn't help but laugh once or twice. But seeing his own hands work the saw blade back and forth on the girl's throat was more than sobering.

His hands now carried the head of the young diner girl. She was pretty, he thought as he held her face in front of his own. Not as pretty as Carol, but decent enough. Then, with the stomach-churning sensation like free falling, Artie was reminded of another haunting memory from his youth...

He was a schoolboy, maybe 11 or 12, and as a special treat, Artie's entire class was to watch a special presentation of the 1949 Disney film, *The Adventures of Ichabod and Mr. Toad*. After lunch that day, the students gathered in the gymnasium and were seated on the floor as their English teacher, Mrs. Carpuglli, set up the projection. He thought about her... Mrs. Carpuglli was a stern old bat with thick glasses, moles on her nose and neck, and a pronounced hunch back. Her large breasts hung down to her waist, and when she walked, they swung before her like soft, flappy pendulums. "*Carpuglli, you sure are ugly!*" the kids would often snicker behind her back. Once or twice, someone had been brave enough to yell it at the woman after she started her car and was leaving the school parking lot.

On this particular day, Artie had drunk two cartons of chocolate milk at lunch and a half gallon of water during morning class. But it wasn't until he was seated on the gymnasium floor that he realized he needed to pee. Mrs. Carpuglli had busted some of the kids for smoking cigarettes in the bathroom during a lecture a few weeks back, and ever since, she was quite strict when it came to potty breaks. Before everyone sat down in the gymnasium, she told the students there would be no bathroom breaks until the film was over. Knowing it was no use asking now, and not wanting to be berated by the ugly Carpuglli, Artie held it in.

Artie sat in the front row, looking up at the white sheet being used as a makeshift screen. The film was in two segments. The first segment, *The Wind in the Willows*, follows J. Thaddeus Toad, Esq., a toad with a profound obsession with motor cars. Artie found this story to be quite amusing and almost humorous, as the protagonist Mr. Toad reminded Artie of his father's obsession with vehicles. He enjoyed the film so much, he nearly forgot how badly he needed to pee.

The second and final segment of the film was an animated telling of *The Legend of Sleepy Hollow*. The first half of the film was enjoyable enough, following the main character, Ichabod Crane, as the charming but silly new schoolmaster of the town. But the ending, featuring the telling of the terrifying tale of the Headless Horseman and the ghostly Horseman's deadly chase of Ichabod through the dark woods, combined with the overfull bladder of a young Arthur Novac, caused him to uncontrollably wet his pants... right there in the front row of the gymnasium. Artie could still remember hiding his crying face both in fear of the Horseman and embarrassment of the yellow puddle starting to grow all around him and the children seated next to him.

When the film ended and the lights were turned on, there was a wave of groans and disgust that dispersed throughout the children, with Artie at the epicenter. His face was leaking tears, his pants were leaking urine, and from that day on, Artie would be known as "Ichabod Crane" to his schoolmates. His new nickname would, without fail, be accompanied by a roar of laughter anytime it was mentioned.

It had been years since then, yet Artie still felt the same intense wave of shame wash over him whenever he thought about it, even now as he held the diner girl's head.

Artie wiped a tear from his eye, and like the Headless Horseman, tucked the diner girl's head under his arm as he made his way into the night.

He moved like a nightcrawler. Through the dark streets he slinked, hiding behind parked cars on the street whenever headlights appeared in front or behind him. He imagined he was a ghost, haunting the night and creeping quietly through the streets. If only he had a horse to ride... but by midnight, Artie was back home, placing the waitress's head neatly inside the freezer next to Martin's.

The two faces were quite a contrast. One, bloody and mangled, adorned with ice crystals like a mountain climber that gets frozen in a snowstorm. The other, fresh and colorful, with smooth skin. Streams of mascara teared down the girl's face, her eyes now frozen in terror. And the last thing she ever saw was the expressionless mask worn by the sleepy guy in the diner who stole a piece of pie as he stormed out.

Artie stood with the freezer door opened wondering what had become of him... The itch had gone, that was true. And he had not thought about the *Terrible Thing* since being in the cemetery with Martin. But he felt like a shell of himself; a vacant vessel running on autopilot, barely aware of the shock he was in. But before the notion of good and evil comes to mind, or the question of whether one is born with a violent heart arises, let it be known that Arthur Novac was not a sadist with a craving for bloodlust, nor was he a preconditioned killer. He was simply a man haunted.

16

MARCUS

OLD FOLKS WAKE UP EARLY…

July 15 ~ Afternoon/Evening

WHEN THE TWO men got back into the truck, the Sheriff pulled out another cigarette. He handed the pack to Marcus. "You sure?" he asked.

Marcus shrugged. "Why not?" he said as he took a cigarette and lit it.

"Good man," said the Sheriff. "Before we get food, we got one more stop to make."

"Lead the way," Marcus said, and blew smoke out his window. His stomach growled again but he told himself it wouldn't be much longer.

The Sheriff took the left at the corner where the house with the caution tape was and continued down the road for about a mile. Then he took another left onto Culver Street, and Marcus could see that the houses of the neighborhood ended up ahead. When they reached the third house from the last, the Sheriff parked his truck, shut off the engine and got out. Marcus followed.

The house was small with a nicely manicured front lawn.

There were no lights on inside. The Sheriff led Marcus around the house to the backyard. There was no fence, just two rocking chairs—one overturned on its side—at the base of a small stone patio, a gas engine-powered lawn mower left sitting in the middle of the backyard, and a garden growing tomatoes, asparagus, and some kind of pepper plants toward the back of the yard.

The backyard looked out over an expanse of dark woods that sat ominously behind the row of houses that lined the neighborhood. Marcus noticed a small clearing to the right. The sun was nearly set now, the faint glow on the horizon made for a particularly beautiful sky. The waxing crescent moon sat overhead toward the East, and many stars were beginning to appear. "Pretty dense back here," he said to the Sheriff, looking into the woods.

The Sheriff pointed to the lawn near the mower. "Two more bodies here not long after the others were found yesterday. Neighbors called it in."

"What time was this?"

"Early morning."

"Did you speak with the neighbor?"

"Of course."

"What'd they say?"

"She said the lawn mower had been running for hours but she couldn't see anyone operating it. So, she came over to see what was going on and found the old lady who lived here torn to shreds. Still in her nightgown."

"What about the husband?" asked Marcus.

The Sheriff shook his head, "not a scratch on him, actually. Coroner said it looks like a heart attack."

"And they were mowing the lawn at sunrise?"

The Sheriff shrugged. "Old folks wake up early."

"Where were they?"

"The old couple? Just laying here in the grass. The lawn mower was still running when my boys got here."

"Yeah, you said that. Any gunshots here?" Marcus asked.

"Nope. No sign of any kind of struggle."

"And nobody saw anything?"

The Sheriff threw his cigarette butt into the yard. "Well, the neighbor who reported this said she awoke to a loud bang, probably some turkey hunter. And she heard a loud thumping on her roof shortly after."

"Turkey hunter?" said Marcus.

"It's turkey season," the Sheriff shook his head and chuckled to himself. "But that could have been anything," he said. "Lots of wildlife out here," he motioned to the dark forest. "Coulda been a turkey roosting, or a vulture. Or even a bobcat. Been known to happen from time to time. Buddy of mine shot one off his roof last winter."

"He shot what off his roof?"

"Bobcat." The Sheriff put his hands in front of him about three feet apart. "'Bout this big."

Marcus looked around. He scanned the woods line again and pointed to the clearing on the right. "What's that opening in the forest over there?" he asked.

"Oh that," said the Sheriff. "That's just an old mine. Been out of operation since '61."

"Can we check it out?"

The Sheriff chuckled. "What for? Place is deserted."

Marcus shrugged. "When's the last time you were there?"

"Beats me. But I'm telling you, Detective, ain't nobody going anywhere near that old place." The Sheriff spit in the grass. "Plus, it's been flooded."

"I'd still like to see it," Marcus said.

The Sheriff looked at the ground and shook his head. "That place gives me the creeps, and it's too dark to be stumbling around down there. Liable to get ourselves killed. Besides, I thought you were hungry." The Sheriff slapped Marcus on the shoulder. "C'mon, let's go get something to eat." And with that, the Sheriff led the way back to his truck.

Marcus began to follow, then looked back over his shoulder at the woods towards the clearing. He heard the unmistakable sound of a baby crying, and called to the Sheriff, "You hear that?"

The Sheriff was walking through the front yard. He reached his truck parked on the street and opened the door. "Hear what?" he shouted back to Marcus.

"That crying noise. Coming from over there," Marcus pointed to the clearing in the distance.

The Sheriff laughed. "You sure are a city boy, huh? That's a coyote, my boy. Maybe a fox." He got in the driver's seat and motioned for Marcus to join him. "Come on, let's get some food."

Marcus stood in the yard listening for the sound, but it had stopped. He took out his notepad, wrote down the word *mine*, then joined the Sheriff in his truck.

17

DARLA
OTHER STUFF…

July 15 ~ Evening/Night

THE THIRD TIME James Hatfield asked her out, Darla finally said yes. But it wasn't really because she wanted to. She mostly wanted him to stop asking. It was embarrassing, after all, because he always made a scene of it. And each time he asked was more grand than the last.

The first time was last year on a Thursday at school during lunch. Right before the bell rang that dismissed the students to their afternoon classes, James stood up on top of the table he and his friends were sitting at and declared his love for Darla to the entire cafeteria. He banged his lunch tray on the table three times and the room went silent. Then he pointed to Darla from across the room and shouted, "Darla Tompkins, I think I love you! Let's go steady!"

Every head in the cafeteria turned toward Darla, who was sitting with her friends in the corner. The silence was eerie, she thought, but the faces were worse. All those eyeballs fixed on her, wide with anticipation and excitement. She wasn't used to that kind of attention, and quite frankly, she didn't like it.

At the time, Darla was a junior at Burnwell High School, and James was a senior. Durning her freshman and sophomore years, Darla went mostly unnoticed. But something had happened over the summer of her junior year, and whatever it was, it made Darla much more popular, especially with the boys. She could feel the eyeballs on her when she walked through the halls, and on more than one occasion she'd turned her head behind her while walking up the steps to see three or four boys staring up from beneath her, smiling, only to turn their eyes back toward the ground and giggle when she caught them.

But she was no fool. She knew what it was those boys had suddenly become so interested in. But her development wasn't her fault. And as a modest girl from a Christian household, she wanted to part in the newfound attention she was receiving. But that was easier said than done when James Hatfield was the admirer.

James was a star of the football team. He was tall and strong with a winning smile. And Darla had to admit, she liked the way his light brown curls flowed out from underneath his helmet when he ran. He was used to getting what he wanted. He had no shame and all the confidence in the world. But Darla had it in her mind that James was a jerk, and therefore, when he declared his love for her to the entire cafeteria that day, she covered her face and excused herself from the table, leaving the cafeteria without so much as a glance back at James.

There was a wave of whispers throughout the room as Darla left. And as she walked quickly down the hall to her next class, he heard James yell jovially, "That's alright! I'll just ask you again tomorrow!" Followed by an eruption of laughter and cheers from the food hall.

And while she may have thought James to be a self-centered, egocentric jock, the next day he proved that he was certainly not a liar.

After the final bell rang on that Friday, Darla and her friends made their way out the front door and into the crisp fall afternoon air. There was a bustle of kids making their way to the buses and bikes and cars in the parking lot. And as soon as Darla stepped foot on the bottom stairs of the school entrance, there were a series of obnoxious honks coming from the red Ford Mustang that everyone knew was James Hatfield's. Once again, all heads turned toward James as he shimmied his torso out of the driver side window and shouted, "Darla Tompkins! Do you reject my love a second time!?"

The eyes of the crowd found Darla again and this time she responded, "Yes I do, James Hatfield!" The crowd laughed, James laughed, and Darla made her way to her bus.

"Very well!" she heard James yell from his car, "Then I'll ask again tonight!" Again, the crowd cheered, James sped off in his Mustang, and Darla boarded her bus without turning around to watch him. That was the second time he asked her out. And nobody saw, but as Darla took her seat on the bus for the ride home, she couldn't help but smile.

That night, James proved again that he was no liar. At the varsity football game, which most of the small town always attended, the cock crowed for a third time.

It was late in the fourth quarter, and Burnwell had just scored the go-ahead touchdown on a deep pass that was caught by none other than James Hatfield himself. After he scored, James ran straight out of the endzone up to the bleachers and down the row that Darla and her friends were sitting in. This time, James didn't say anything. He just handed the ball to Darla and winked. The referee threw a flag for excessive celebration, and James hurried back down to the field in a wave of cheers and atta-boys from the crowd.

Third time's a charm, Darla thought, because for some reason, it worked. After the football game that night, Darla had waited for James in the school parking lot. And ever since, they'd been going steady.

That was nearly nine months ago, and Darla reminisced on the early charm of her boyfriend as he drove her down the country backroads on this mid-summer night.

"Can you believe we've been dating for almost nine months?" she asked, sitting in the passenger seat of James's Mustang.

The radio was loud and the windows were down as James sped through the windy road that led through the forest outside of town.

"What'd you say!?" he shouted over the noise.

Darla turned down the radio, "I said we've been dating for nine months!"

James nodded in some kind of false fascination. "Huh," he said. "Feels like longer." He turned the radio back up and speed forward, the engine revving through the trees.

When they reached the overlook that sat nestled atop the hill in the woods, James pulled his car into the small gravel lot next to the road and turned off the ignition and headlights. The overlook looked out over an expanse of dark West Virgina mountains, and stars could be seen above the faint orange glow left by the sun as it was setting.

"James," Darla said. "We missed the sunset." She folder her arms and scowled.

"I'm sorry, babe. I had to catch the end of the Orioles game." Darla glared at him, then back toward the overlook. "We're one game out of the pennant race!" James said. He put his hand on her shoulder.

She shook it off. "I told you I really wanted to see the sunset tonight. The sky looked beautiful."

"Not as beautiful as you."

"Oh save it," Darla said. "Besides, you're a man now. You can't spend all your time watching sports."

James bent his head forward. "I don't spend *all* my time watching sports," he said quietly. "I just graduated a couple months ago. And I'm gonna start working the mines next week."

Darla still sat with her arms folded. "Well, at least that outta keep you busy," she said.

"Maybe you could keep me busy til then," James said as he leaned over to kiss her.

Darla laughed softly then met his lips with hers. The woods were quiet, aside from the sound of crickets echoing in the night, and the only other sound was the shuffling of the two in the passenger seat. They made out for a minute or two, then James's hand went from Darla's breast to between her legs. She caught it and moved it up on to her knee.

James stopped kissing her and sighed. "C'mon babe. There's no one around."

"You know how I feel James. I wanna wait til we're married."

James backed away from her and sat back in the driver's seat. He put his hands to his face and rubbed his forehead.

"Or at least until I graduate," Darla said, reaching out to touch James's shoulder.

"That's like a year from now!" James said loudly.

Darla removed her hand from his shoulder and looked between her feet.

"Je-sus," James said under his breath. "This just ain't fair."

Darla took a deep breath. "Maybe we can do... other stuff," she said quietly.

James perked up. "Oh yeah? Like what?"

"Well..." Darla slid her hand between James's legs and undid the zipper of his jeans slowly. "I can think of some—"

BANG-Screeeee!

Something big had fallen onto the roof of the car and scratched the metal when it hit.

Darla pulled her hand back. "What was that?" she asked.

"What was what? I didn't hear anything." James reached for her hand and moved it back over his crotch.

"Stop," Darla said. "Listen." Something wasn't right. The woods were completely silent now, even the crickets had stopped chirping. Suddenly, Darla felt frightened. She couldn't shake the feeling that something was watching them. "Let's get out of here," she whispered. "I want to go home."

James laughed. "Not yet," he said. He pulled her close to him and put his hand on the back of her head. He pushed her head down next to the steering wheel. "Where were we?"

She tried to move her head away and sit up, but he held her tightly. "Stop," she said again. "I want to go."

"You're joking," said James. "There's nothing out there. Now come on." He pressed her head down further and she tried to fight. His grip was tight on the back her head and it was starting to hurt where he was pulling her hair.

She thrashed and squirmed and started hitting his leg with her fist. Then she heard the sound of scratching metal come from the roof of the car again, this time louder and unmistakable. James threw her head off him and into the passenger side door.

"The fuck did you do?" James asked harshly.

Darla was crying now, holding the side of her head where it had hit the door. "I didn't do anything," she cried softly.

They sat in silence for another moment. The night as still and silent as the grave. Then the car moved, and both Darla and James jumped and screamed. There was another brief sound of scratching metal, and a large dark object appeared in front of the windshield. In a blink, it was gone, but Darla saw a huge shadow in front of them flying over the overlook. She screamed again and pointed to it. James flashed his headlights on to catch a glimpse of the thing, but it was nowhere to be found. But for a moment, they could both hear the soft sound of wings flapping against the sky, then the sound was gone and replaced by the crickets in the woods once again.

They sat in silence. Then Darla said quietly, "please take me home."

"Way ahead of ya," James said as he started the engine.

As they drove, Darla noticed he was speeding faster than he'd ever driven her before, and h had a look of pure terror on his handsome face. A look she'd never seen on him before. She closed her eyes, said a silent prayer, and vowed never to speak about this night ever again.

18

ARTIE

LIKE THAT...

July 15 ~ Night

HE COULD SMELL the flowers in the air and taste the honey on his lips. The bed sheets were black and the bed itself was firm. Almost too firm, like hardwood. But his knees didn't hurt as they pressed hard onto the bed. Carol was sprawled out on her hands and knees in front of him, her back arched. She was naked except for a pair of red panties, her hair in pigtail braids. Artie placed his hands on the smooth white skin of her butt. "Go ahead," she told him. He couldn't see her face; they were both facing the wall. Artie took the lace of her underwear in his fingers and slowly pulled them down her backside and let them fall to her knees. He got in position to put himself inside her. His heart was beating. His mind was racing. It didn't make sense on the surface; too much at stake. Her with the loss of her husband; him with the loss of his mind. But it felt good, and Artie hadn't felt this way for as long as he could remember. He moved his hips closer, but instead of penetrating her, he found himself sitting atop her like a rider mounts a steed.

Then he heard her say again, "go ahead, Arthur," and he

grabbed her braids; one in each hand and pulled tightly. "Yeah, like that," she said. He pulled again, and she moaned.

He tried to speak but couldn't; tried to move, but she moved for him. They were in the woods now, him riding on her naked back. He steered her through the trees. If he pulled on her left braid, she turned left, and the same for the right. It was tremendous. They danced through trees, setting them ablaze as they rode by. Artie could feel the wind on his face, and he could feel himself smile, even laugh, as they rode. After speeding through a maze of trails, pulling Carol's braids this way and that, they reached a clearing at the edge of the woods, and he let go of her hair.

"Don't stop now, Arthur," he heard Carol say from below him. But his palms were burning. He looked down at his hands to see them covered in blood, and her braids where he gripped them were blood-soaked. Then Artie heard a cracking of twigs, and out of the forest, another steed stepped into the clearing.

Its eyes were burning red embers, as if the fires of hell itself burned inside them. Its body was black or shadowed from what Artie could see. And from its back flapped large black wings like a gothic Pegasus.

Mounted upon it sat a headless figure with indiscernible features. The winged beast with the red eyes turned to the side, and Artie could see the headless rider carrying something in its hand. Artie pulled on Carol's braids to move closer, but she didn't move. Then the beast began to approach, and after a few steps, Artie could see what the rider was carrying: it was the head of Carol's oldest daughter. She had her hair done in the same style of braided pigtails as her mother atop whom Artie still sat. The beast stopped walking, and the headless rider began to whip the girl's head by the braid like a cowboy does with a lasso.

Artie heard a loud bang, and the beast took off. It ran away from him with the headless rider still swinging the girl's head as it moved. It ran toward the end of the clearing and stopped at an entrance that descended into the ground. Then Artie realized where it was heading. The creature looked back at him, those huge red eyes staring into Artie's and freezing him. His mouth was dry; he couldn't swallow. The headless rider let the girl's head fall to the ground, but still held her by a single braid. Artie heard Carol scream from beneath him, and the beast walked down into the darkness, its rider dragging the girl's head as it descended into the abandoned Dribble Creek mine.

Artie stared into the black entrance, the sound of the beast's footsteps echoing more and more faintly as it rode on. And out from the darkness of the doorway, Artie saw a pale white hand reach out to him, and the curling of long, spidery fingers that hadn't seen the sun in years. He never saw anything more than the hand, but he knew, deep down, it was something familiar, beckoning him to come inside.

MARCUS

DO YOU LIKE THE BEATLES?

July 15 ~ Night

THE RIDE to the diner was a quiet one. The Sheriff smoked another cigarette on the way, Marcus declined one. He wasn't much of a smoker these days. Sure, he'd had plenty of cigarettes in his youth, trying to be cool around the older kids on the block. But mostly, smoking just gave him a headache now. And he didn't like the way his breath smelled after smoking. Though he must admit, for some reason, he did enjoy the faint smell of smoke that lingered on his fingertips and shirt collar. It reminded him of his mother.

On the truck radio, they listened to the voice of Casey Kasem perform his spoken word recording of "Letter from Elaina". The story spoke of a woman who meet George Harrison of the Beatles after a concert in San Francisco. The Sheriff chuckled and smiled softly during Kasem's rendition.

"You ever been to San Francisco?" Marcus asked.

The Sheriff laughed quietly again, "Oh no. I doubt you'll ever find me in California." He turned the volume on the radio up just a hair. "I do like the Beatles though, I must say." He looked at Marcus, "What about you?"

"I told you, never been West of Richmond."

"No," the Sheriff said. "Do you like the Beatles?"

"Oh. Yeah, sure," he lied.

The Sheriff turned up the radio a bit more, and they continued their drive without speaking.

When they arrived at the diner it was nighttime. The sun had fully set, and the moon and stars were bright in the night sky. As the Sheriff pulled his truck into the parking lot, a man with glasses wearing a shirt and tie emerged from behind the diner building and began banging excitedly on the hood of the truck.

"Jesus Christ! Thank God!" The man said. He was nearly out of breath, in a state of full panic. "Help! Help, Sheriff!"

"Take it easy, Jeffrey. What's the matter?" The Sheriff opened the door and got out. Marcus watched from inside the truck.

"It's Shelly... she's—" The man curled over and vomited, spewing chunks on the door of the truck and the Sheriff's shoes.

"Aw for Chrissake, Jeff!" The Sheriff took a step back and wiped his feet on the curb of the sidewalk.

The man in glasses stood up and wiped his mouth with the back of his hand, then his tie. "Sorry Sheriff, but Shelly's been killed!" He bent over and started to dry heave again, but nothing came out.

"What do you mean?" asked the Sheriff, placing a hand on the man's back.

The man stayed hunched over, his hands on his knees, and pointed toward the alley behind the diner where he'd come running from. "Over there," he said between breaths, still looking at the ground.

The Sheriff pulled out his flashlight, clicked it on, and began walking toward the alley. Marcus got out of the truck and followed him, careful not to step in the fresh vomit.

He walked quickly, trying to catch up to the Sheriff, whose silhouette was illuminated by the flashlight. The only thing Marcus could see were the bricks of the walls of the alley. Then the Sheriff stopped, and Marcus heard him say, "Dear God in heaven." Marcus caught up to him and peered over his shoulder.

The Sheriff's flashlight was pointed at the base of the alley wall, where sat a headless corpse in a server's apron, arms sprawled out to the sides, surrounded by a pool of blood. The body sat upright; back against the wall, legs stretched out in front with the feet turned outward. The Sheriff reached out toward the body with his left hand.

"Don't touch it!" yelled Marcus. "Get squad cars out here immediately, we need to section off this area now. Start at the parking lot. Close the diner. Tell the manager to send everyone home."

"Dear God," said the Sheriff again. "Little Shelly McGuire."

"Sheriff," Marcus said, looking him in the face. "I need you to get your boys down here."

"Right," said the Sheriff. He handed Marcus his flashlight. "You're the boss, Detective. My radio's in the truck."

The Sheriff began to walk back toward his truck. "Sheriff," Marcus called after him. "Is this what you mean by 'mutilate the bodies'? Like the others?"

"No, Detective. This is something else."

20

ARTIE

GOOD FOR YOU...

July 16 ~ Morning

WHEN ARTIE AWOKE, he threw the covers off himself and onto the floor. He hurriedly scampered to get dressed. There was blood on his shirt, so he put on a clean flannel from his closet. The jeans he'd been wearing were hanging off the side of the bed. He picked them up and examined them; no blood stains to be found. He smelled them, and determined they smelled fresh enough. So, he put them on, splashed some cold water on his face, strapped on his boots, and headed for the front door. He was alert; more focused than he'd been in days, and more sober. So sober that he remembered to close the cellar door on his way toward the kitchen (there were no sounds of swinging ropes). And (he winced) sober enough to remember the fresh-faced girl's head that sat in his freezer as he walked by it.

He was headed to Carol's house. She was in trouble; he could feel it. Birds were singing and the morning sun was shining brightly as he walked down the street. He walked quickly, nearly running, and as he neared the edge of town, about two blocks from Carol's house on the far corner, Dave's head caught up with him.

"Why the hurry, Artie?" it said.

"Carol."

The head chuckled. "On the hunt for some morning pussy. Good for you."

"That's not what I'm after."

"Why not? I told you I didn't mind."

Artie walked even faster now, "She's in trouble."

"Ah, I see. Come to play the savior then, eh?" Dave's voice was more serious now.

Artie didn't answer. He walked with strict determination, trying not to pay attention to the grisly floating balloon beside him.

As he approached Carol's front lawn, Dave's head stopped following him. "Don't be a hero now, Artie," it called after him. "Gonna get yourself killed."

Artie ran up the porch steps and banged hard on the front door. A moment later, Carol opened the door. She'd been crying.

"Arthur," she said as she wiped her eyes with the back of her hand. "What are you doing here?"

"I thought you might need my help. I had a dream something happened." Carol opened the door further to let Artie inside.

"Oh. Well—"

"What is it?" Artie asked.

"It's Theo. She never came home last night." Carol began to cry again. "She was supposed to be grounded but she snuck out. Dani saw her out the window."

Artie put his arms around her. "It's okay," he said patting her back gently. They stood in the middle of the living room.

"I saw it again." A tiny voice came from the hallway near the kitchen. It was Dani, the younger daughter.

"Saw what?" asked Artie.

"The bad man. With the eyes. That's been watching." Artie let go of Carol and both adults looked at the child.

"When did you see it?"

"Last night. After Theo left. It followed her."

"Oh God, Arthur," said Carol. "What is she talking about?"

"Where did they go?" he asked the little girl.

She pointed out the kitchen window. Artie walked over to the window and pulled back the curtain. The kitchen window faced the woods, and Artie felt his stomach drop when he saw the clearing in the distance.

"Baby, I don't understand." Carol bent down and took her daughter's hand softly. The girl didn't speak again. She just looked at Artie, those big screaming blue eyes, sad and afraid.

Artie had seen this coming. He knew what he had to do before he left his house. But the thought of it made his throat feel dry and sticky.

"What's going on?" Carol asked her daughter again.

"I know where she is," said Artie quietly, looking out the window toward the woods. He walked back to the living room and Carol stood up. "I'll go get her," Artie said. "Bring her back."

"Arthur..."

"Call the police," he said. "Tell them to go to Dribble Creek. I'm going. Before it's too late."

"What—" Carol started, but before she could finish, Artie was out the door. Out the kitchen window she could see him running through the field towards the clearing in the woods.

21

ARTIE

THE BECKONING...

July 16 ~ Morning

THE FIELD behind the Meyerowitz's house hadn't been designated for any crops yet this year. And because of this, it was overgrown with weeds, wildflowers, and tiny shrubs hoping to make a long-term residency.

Artie's boots made heavy footsteps through the field, and he found himself following what must have been a deer trail; long blades of grass parted on either side that twisted and turned in a random zig zag, but ultimately heading toward the opening in the woods at the far end of the field.

Or so Artie thought...

As the trail went on, he was being lead further left, into the central part of the forest, thick with deciduous trees whose canopy shone brightly in the summer sun, but whose innards formed a stark contrast, a dark and foreboding maze of tree trunks that all blended into black the further in you looked.

He was nearly halfway across the field now, and Artie had to keep turning his head to the right to keep an eye on his destination; the entrance to the Dribble Creek Colliery. When his neck began to ache, he decided to abandon the deer trail and charge headlong into the wild growth of the unkept meadow.

Walking through the tall grass slowed his progress a bit, but Artie was at least headed straight for the mine entrance now.

His legs made a *swish-swish* sound as he walked, creating his own kind of pathway, and the briars that lay hidden within the grass hitchhiked their way onto his pant legs and boot laces.

As he neared the clearing, he emerged from the meadow and stood maybe fifty yards from the entrance of the mine. Again, he was disturbed by the contrast of the bright sunlight casting down upon the meadow and the complete blackness that lay trapped within the rectangular borders of the mine entrance; a descending nightmare of darkness that stood before him.

He closed his eyes, took a deep breath, and stepped forward. But he didn't find even footing... Instead, his right foot had stepped into a groundhog hole and twisted sharply to the left, causing almost all of his weight to fall on his ankle which was now in direct contact with the ground. He stumbled forward and yelped as he fell, and his lip hit his knee, leaving a small gash that began bleeding instantly.

Cursing quietly to himself, Artie got to his knees and touched his lip. He could taste blood in his mouth and saw it on his fingers. As he wiped his hand on his shirt, he heard the unmistakable echo of laughter in front of him. It was a hallow sound, that disappeared when he raised his head.

He stayed here on his knees for a moment staring into the depths of the mine entrance, listening. But there was no more sound, save for the birds and bugs that flew by and buzzed around him.

He shook his head and got to his feet. Then he saw, from out of the darkness of the mine, the tip of a white finger protrude. And Artie stood frozen as the finger curled toward the darkness, beckoning him inside, just like he'd seen the night before in his dream.

22

MARCUS

ONE OF THE LUCKIEST DISASTERS IN HISTORY...

July 16 ~ Early Morning

IT WAS NEARLY 5AM by the time Marcus left the crime scene behind the diner, and his eyelids had never felt heavier. It was nearly impossible to believe that just 24 hours ago, he was dreaming peacefully under the stars next to the ocean, the soothing sound of the waves lulling him to sleep. But now those stars had been replaced with flashing lights, and the waves gave way to police sirens.

He stumbled into the modest and musty motel room the Sheriff had booked for him and threw himself on the bed. He lay there fully clothed in his suit and tie, his shiny black shoes hanging off the edge of the bed. He wanted nothing more than to drift off into a deep sleep, but his mind was racing. It had been nothing but utter chaos since his arrival in Burnwell, and he doubted his superiors had any idea it was this bad.

As tired as he was, Marcus Wrathmore had never been able to sleep in the deep silence you hear in a small town like Burnwell. Back home in Baltimore, the streets had been alive all through the night. Cars passing outside his bedroom window every few seconds with an occasional *honk* or loud stereo, some-times an ambulance or fire truck blaring sirens, all illuminated by streetlamps and creating an almost bizarre feeling of safety, or at least, *movement*. The same was true for his new home in Washington DC. And in Rodanthe he had the waves. But here in Burnwell, the silence was ominous and deafening, and the more he focused on hearing nothing, the more he heard the ringing in his ears, piercing his consciousness like a pinprick keeping him awake.

Unable to take it any longer, he rolled over and turned on the old box TV at the foot of the bed. It was on the local morning news, and they were covering some election fraud or another that was taking place in Charleston, just an hour or so up the road. This was certainly boring enough to do the trick and put him to sleep, but just as Marcus was drifting off, the next news story caught his attention, albeit unwillingly.

It was a brief report on the anniversary of the Tragedy of the Dribble Creek Colliery. Marcus sat up, his shoes still hanging off the bed. The voice of the reporter, a middle-aged woman with brown hair and glasses, was soft, but professional, in that unmis-takable West Virginia accent Marcus had heard since he arrived in this town:

"Five years ago today, the Dribble Creek Colliery Mine collapsed in what has been called "one of the luckiest mining disasters in histo-ry..." Around 3AM On Sunday, July 16, 1961, a support pillar in one of the far Western tunnels collapsed causing a minor bump *and a brief rock burst.*

The term "lucky" has been used to describe the scene because as far as mining catastrophes go, this one is considered light. According to reports, early morning shifts on the weekends had just been scaled back to appease the workers' union who was fighting for more relaxed hours, especially on Sundays. As it turns out, only three miners were working in the West tunnel at the time of the collapse, though tragi-

cally, two of the three, Lawrence Winters and Matthew Gulbright, were confirmed dead. The lone survivor, Charles M. Sanders, of Burnwell, West Virginia, fought for closure of the Dribble Creek mine in response to this failure, and it was granted just two months after the collapse.

But though the Dribble Creek mine has been abandoned for nearly five years now, the county has yet to flood the mine, a common practice when a mine is considered officially closed. WBGN has reached out to inquire when we might expect the flooding to be done, but no time frame has been released.

For WBGN News, I'm Rachel Tethers."

Marcus was awake now, he turned off the TV and rubbed his eyes. *So, the mine wasn't flooded after all.* But why would the Sheriff tell him it was? Marcus had a knack for going places he shouldn't, and that very instinct had helped elevate his status as a crime solver. It was this inexplicable hunch that allowed him to scope out with near certainty the locations of the drug dens the biggest dealers were dwelling in back in the city. And for some reason, this abandoned mine was giving him a similar feeling. But to go there would be in direct opposition to the Sheriff. And though that meant little to Marcus in the grand scheme of his duties as an investigator, he couldn't help but like the Sheriff. He'd been more welcoming than anyone else in this town, and if Marcus could find a way to explore the mine without ruffling any feathers, he supposed that would be for the best.

He reached for the drawer in the bedside table and pulled out the phonebook. He flipped to the *S* section and found *Sanders, Charles* in a matter of minutes. The time was 5:58 AM. Marcus figured he would rest for 30 minutes or so, then give the lone survivor of the Dribble Creek disaster a call.

23

ARTIE

THE DESCENT…

July 16 ~ Morning

THE DESCENT into the mine was a slow one.

Artie took large, lanky steps at first, limping slightly on his twisted right ankle, but his gait became increasingly smaller as he marched forward. He'd been counting his steps in his head since he entered the mine fully. He was now on step 48, though each "step" merely inched him forward. Turning his head every few steps, the bright light of the meadow behind him shrunk more and more, and the temperature was dropping with each step forward.

There was no white finger, no figure at all. Only the sound of dripping water that echoed off the walls in a slow rhythm and the sound of his heart beating through his chest, a pounding like a drum in his ears.

What a fool he was, he thought. He'd brought no weapon, not even a flashlight. He was willingly walking into a cold, dark cell that ate light like a black hole. The very same cell that had killed his father years before.

54. 55. 56. 57.

He turned to check the light behind him again and found it even smaller. The illumination couldn't reach him, and he now stood in pitch black darkness. Reaching out, he touched the wall with his right hand. Cold and wet. Then moved his hand up to the ceiling. It was just above his head. He was being squeezed. The walls were moving closer. He knew this would happen. The mine eats... His left hand felt the wall on the other side, and sure enough, it too was closing in. He soon realized he could no longer hear his heartbeat.

All he could hear were his breaths, wheezing in and out, struggling to steady. Artie fell to his knees, one hand on his chest, the other on his throat. His breath was hot, and the cold air he inhaled stung his lungs like a hundred tiny hornets.

Faster and faster he wheezed. Still on his knees, he spun himself toward the fading light of the entrance. He tried to stand, but his bum ankle buckled when he tried to rise, and he fell flat on his stomach.

He could see the long blades of grass swaying in the wind in the distance, out of reach like a prisoner watching children play in the park from his barred window. His breathing slowed, and his eyelids began to droop. Then the piercing light of the sun was blocked by something. But Artie never saw what, his eyes had already closed.

24

MARCUS

STRANGE THINGS ALL THE TIME...

July 16 ~ Morning

AT 8AM ON THE DOT, Marcus pulled up the address Charles Sanders had given him over the phone. It was about what Marcus had imagined a retired coal miner's house might look like. A small trailer on the edge of town, backed up as close to the little river that flowed behind it as possible. The grass was overgrown to such a point that it no longer looked like a yard, more like a field or meadow that had no intention of being manicured. The front porch, if you could call it that, was covered by large, plastic squares of old Coca-Cola signage that might be seen outside a gas station or convenience store. From the "roof" hung strange looking ornaments from several strings; some kind of herb or root that Marcus didn't recognize, and a few pieces of bone, or maybe antler, Marcus couldn't tell.

He carefully avoided all the hanging knickknacks and knocked on the door, and a voice from inside the trailer invited him to step in.

The inside was slightly more inviting than the outside. The trailer felt even smaller from within, and everything was carpet.

Rugs were hung on the walls and ceiling to create a bizarre kind of cushiness to the place.

There were only two rooms, if you could call them that, and they were separated by a shield of hanging beads that nearly reached the floor, hanging just an inch or two above the ground. It was dark inside, and Marcus's eyes had barely adjusted when he heard a voice to his right say, "Well, I suppose you'll be wanting to sit down."

In the back right corner Marcus saw a lamp flick on. A man with a long white beard with long white hair to match sat in a corduroy lazy boy. Both his beard and hair were braided poorly but with style, and Marcus admired the man for trying, though his aunt could have done wonders to those braids if she were here. *Good luck getting her out here*, Marcus thought. He nodded gratefully and made his way over to the man sitting in the chair. It took three steps to reach the corner.

"Detective Wrathmore," he said, extending his hand. The man with white hair looked puzzled for a moment, then took his hand and shook it weakly but didn't look Marcus in the eye. "Mr. Sanders, I presume?"

The man made a grunt of confirmation and motioned Marcus to the sit in the weathered chair that sat across from the one he was sitting in.

"Thanks," Marcus said as he took his seat. "I'm sorry to have called you so early in the morning, it's just that—"

"I wasn't asleep," said the man.

"Right. It's just that I saw you on the news and thought you might be able to help me."

The man made another grunting noise.

"You see, Mr. Sanders—"

"Charles," the man said.

"Excuse me," said Marcus. "You see, Charles, I'm here on a special request, investigating some strange activity that's been going on around here lately. Do you know what I'm referring to?"

Charles shrugged.

"Have you seen anything strange lately?"

Charles spit into a mug that was sitting on the little table beside his chair. "See strange things all the time."

"Such as?" Marcus asked.

"Such as a black boy wearing a suit in my living room."

Marcus smiled. It was only a matter of time. He held his tie out in front of his eyes and looked at it. "You like it? Gotta look the part, you know."

Charles grunted, then spit into the mug again.

"I suppose you didn't wear many suits in your line of work," Marcus said jovially. "In the mines, I mean."

Charles didn't say anything. He had yet to look Marcus in the face.

Marcus cleared his throat. "That's actually why I'm here," he said. "I wanted to ask you about Dribble Creek."

Then the man did look Marcus in the face, and his eyes shown with what Marcus could only imagine was the faintest bit of interest.

"You see, Mr. Sa—I'm sorry—Charles, I've been an investigator for a while now, and I know a hunch when I feel one. And ever since I've been in this town—which hasn't been very long haha—I have to say, I've been interested in that old mine. It seems to be the perfect place for a ne'er-do-well to abide, but I'm getting cold water poured over the idea when I approach it."

Charles spit into the mug and smiled. His teeth—the few he had left—were brown and crooked. "Always strange things in that mine. Always."

Marcus shifted in his seat. "What do you mean? The collapse?"

Charles nodded. "Mhm. Even before. Always heard things. Saw things once or twice." He spit again.

"What kind of things?"

"Critters."

"Like squirrels? Bats?"

Charles shook his head. "Critters, we called 'em. Some folks called 'em goblins."

Marcus wrinkled his face. "What, like elves?"

Charles shrugged. "Don't know. Never talked much. But they made noises. Sometimes like a baby cryin' sounded like. From deep in the mine tunnels."

Marcus swallowed uncomfortably. "And you saw these... These critters?"

"Once or twice with the flash. But they didn't stick 'round long. Mostly noises. 'Specially after we blasted. Found footprints, too."

"Really?"

"Foreman said they was a bird footprints. Fuckin' moron."

Marcus took out his notepad and a pen. "And what did these critters look like when you spotted them?"

"Hard to say. Only saw 'em for a second. But they were white as a sheet. And tiny, 'bout ye high." Charles held his hand out in front of his knee, about two or three feet off the ground. "They had big ears, I think. Or wings maybe comin' out their back. And big black eyes. Shone red kinda when I put the light on 'em."

"And when did you start seeing these things?"

"Whole time we was diggin'. They were there before us. Inna caves."

"Caves?"

Charles laughed. "You city slickers think you know everythin' but you don't. There's things out here in these parts. Things that been here a long time. And they don't always like diggin'.

Them other things that come from the caves, too. Not just little critters. Bigger, so they say."

"Such as?"

"Never seen nothin' but a couple critters. Just heard stories."

"From other miners?"

Charles nodded.

"Before the Dribble Creek collapse?"

"Wasn't no collapse," Charles said shaking his head.

"What do you mean?" asked Marcus.

"I put them braces in that wall myself. We all did. And we was the best crew in that damn place. It was sturdy enough alright."

"You and uh," Marcus checked his notepad, "Winters? And Matthew Gulbright?"

"And Benny."

"Benny?"

Charles chuckled. "They don't talk about Benny on the news, do they?" He laughed a full laugh, showing the wad of chewing tobacco nestled under his brown teeth.

"I don't know what you mean."

"He was in our crew. Benjamin Novac. We called him Benny. Best damn drill operator I ever saw."

Marcus wrote the name *Novac* down in his notebook. "What do you mean about the news?"

"He was there that day, but the news don't say it."

"I don't understand."

"Fuckin' mining company," Charles said and spit again. "Union was fighting 'em back then, you see. Told 'em to cut back on weekend hours."

"Right," replied Marcus. "I did hear that on the news."

"But they didn't cut back. Did you hear that on the news, Mr. Smartypants?"

Marcus shook his head.

"Damn right. They didn't cut back. Only on paper they said *3 Man Crew on Sundays*... But it was always four men anyway. Just the fourth got rotated out on the schedule and got paid cash on days he "wasn't" scheduled. We didn't hate it, cash payment worked good for us just fine. But when that tunnel fell, coal company buried it."

Marcus looked at Charles, waiting to see some kind of smile after a pretty well-placed pun, but he saw none. He looked back at his notes. "So, all three—Winters, Gulbright, and Novac died in that collapse?"

"I told you, was no collapse!"

"I'm sorry, Charles. I'm just trying to figure out what happened."

"Why the fuck you askin' about all this shit anyway? I told my story already. Told the po-lice, the news, anyone who'd listen. But nobody goddamn did."

"I'm listening, Charles."

"It's too late. Mine's closed, but they waitin' to open it again after I die, I figure. Then no one left will be shoutin' about this and that."

"So what happened that day, Charles?"

Charles spit into his mug. "It was early mornin'. Benny was down in the back, hackin' away at some stubborn rock that wouldn't give. Rest of us was haulin' a load back to the loadin' zone, then we heard a methane pop. Like *pop!* But that was normal. Happened from time to time. Usually very small, harmless. So we hollered out to Benny, make sure he was okay. No reply. We called again. Then we heard him screamin', like he was being attacked by somethin', and we could see his light flickerin' off the walls, like he was running or jumpin' around. I was in the front pullin' the cart, Lawrence and Matt were on the rear and were closer to Benny, so they went runnin' to see what all the fuss was about. When they rounded the corner I couldn't see 'em, but I heard somethin' crash. Somethin' thrown or mashed into the tunnel wall back there, and I heard the bracin' snap, then the roof came down, and I tried to holler at 'em but a cloud of dust came at my face and all around. I couldn't see, could hardly breathe. I start coughin' somethin' fierce. Then I ran out to get the foreman. We came back a few minutes later, but by the time we got around the cart, the walls had come down. A few hours later they pulled out Lawrence and Matt, but no Benny. I kept askin' but got no answers from nobody. Then they told me I needed to retire and gave me a pretty pension. I told 'em to go to Hell. After a few months of fightin' they shut the mine down. Haven't reopened it since."

Marcus put his notepad down on his leg and rubbed his temple. "Wait a second. So, you're saying there was no collapse, but rather... some kind of attack?"

"I'm sayin' it didn't happen the way they said it did. Tried to blame us for poor structurin', but that just ain't true. I know it ain't."

"What could have attacked Mr. Novac? Er—Benny?"

Charles shrugged. "Beats me. But I told 'em no chance in Hell I was goin' back in that mine. And no one else should either."

"And you think there's still activity down there?"

"What did I just say, boy? I don't mess 'round there no more."

Marcus stood and extended his hand once more. "Thanks for your time, Charles. You've been a big help."

Charles took his hand but didn't stand. Marcus headed for the door and opened it, and as he was walking out, Charles called to him, "Detective, whatever you do, be useful." Marcus nodded and shut the door behind him.

25

ARTIE
THE FOLLOWING...

July 16 ~ Mid-Morning/Midday

THERE WAS A SHUFFLING SOUND, like something—many things—moving all around him. It sounded like mice scurrying about at night. Artie couldn't tell if it was night. He couldn't tell if his eyes were open, if he'd been blindfolded, or if he'd just plain gone blind. He was laying on his stomach, his head turned to the side. The shuffling around him continued. Slowly, he moved his hand to touch his face, no blindfold. When he moved, the scurrying around him stopped, and Artie could hear only the soft echo of dripping water. Even slower still, he moved his arm back down to his side. As he lay on his stomach, he could feel something small and solid between his left thigh and the rocky ground. Placing his hand under his leg, he felt the outside of the object through the fabric of his jeans. Then he reached his hand inside his pocket and grasped the thing that had been in there for days: Martin's lighter.

He kept his hand inside his pocket and lay flat on his stomach, listening...

Nothing. No more scurrying, only the *drip drip* of the water.

Artie pulled the lighter out slowly and brought it to his face. With the first flick, the flame ignited in front of him, and Artie had to shut his eyes tight. For a moment, the light was more blinding than the darkness had been. In the moments that his eyes began to adjust, he was able to make out the flame itself, dancing silently, and the glistening water on the walls of the mine; walls much closer together in this section compared to where he'd entered. So close, Artie realized that his left elbow was against the far wall, and his right was touching the adjacent wall.

Then he noticed two smaller, identical flames dancing on either side of the larger one in his hand. He was looking at it, but his brain couldn't process it. Or maybe... it *wouldn't* process it. His brain wouldn't let him. But whether he acknowledged it or not, what he was seeing sat before him all the same.

Just beyond the lighter in his hand, merely inches away from his own face, were large, smooth, black eyes staring back into his own. The eyes themselves were nearly as wide as Artie's hand, and the light that shone off them showed greyish white skin that surrounded the eyes. The eyes were like pools of black painted onto a white canvas of a featureless face. The black eyes made up most of the head, and only a small slit sat centered beneath them like the penciled smile of a stick figure.

Once he was able to take it in, Artie tried to let out a yell, but what came out was more like a squeak. And the next thing he knew, the creature with the big black eyes turned and ran. It was small, about as tall as Artie was lying on the ground. And when the thing scurried away behind him, Artie saw movement in the light. More of them were along the walls, a few stood in the center of the tunnel. They all had grey skin with huge, smooth black eyes. They sat there looking at him, and Artie put out the light and tried to stand.

He was able to stand up about halfway before his head

smacked the ceiling hard and he got back down to his knees. He flicked the lighter again and saw the tiny creatures had moved a bit but weren't approaching him. He stood up again and hunched over, his head lightly grazing the ceiling this time. A drop of icy water fell from the rock ceiling down the back of his neck and sent a shiver up his spine.

The creatures then formed a kind of line in front of him, or perhaps more of a barricade. Struggling, Artie turned himself around and held the lighter in front of him. The line of creatures that were on his rear parted, and half of them began scurrying their way down the dark corridor. They walked upright on two legs, with two tiny arms swinging by their sides. More from behind Artie appeared beneath his feet, and they too started down the corridor. Artie took a dry swallow, looked behind him once more, and saw nothing. The entrance he'd come in was nowhere to be found. He was lost, nearly blind, and completely unarmed. So, he did the only thing he could: He followed the tiny creatures into the dark, still half hunched over, his back already beginning to ache.

26

MARCUS

PROCEED WITH CAUTION...

July 16 ~ Morning

BY THE TIME he realized he was still sitting in his car outside Charlie Sanders's house with his face in his hands, the sun was rising high, as was the temperature on another hot summer day.

He'd been digesting all the things Mr. Sanders had told him about the abandon mine. Things that shouldn't happen like having extra labor undocumented each and every weekend... And things that *couldn't* happen, like tiny, white "critters"—as Charles called them—that lived in, or at least frequented, the old mine tunnels.

Marcus rubbed his eyes and finally turned on the ignition. Then heard the two-way radio the Sheriff had given him: *"Detective Wrathmore, come in—over."*

It was the Sheriff. "Wrathmore here—over."

"Where are you, Detective? I'm at the hotel now looking for you —over."

"Apologies, Sheriff. Went for a morning drive—over."

"Enough joyrides, Detective. Got a possible kidnapping/missing

persons reported a few minutes ago by telephone. A Mrs. Meyrowitz said her daughter is missing. 663 Dribble Creek Drive—over."

"Dribble Creek? Like the mine, Sheriff?"

Silence...

"Over," Marcus said.

"That's the one. Edge of town, Northwest. Think you can find it alright? —over."

"Yessir. Be there right away—over."

"Detective, proceed with caution and arrive armed. Caller said a Mr. Arthur Novac is at the scene to "help". He's a suspect in the diner waitress murder; known to frequent that place and was seen by multiple witnesses loitering outside the building that night.

"Mr. Novac is also the last person to have seen the caller's husband, Dave Meyrowitz, and a Mr. Martin Brandt alive. Both of whom are missing and suspected dead—over."

"Any connection to Novac with the Culver Street family massacre? —over."

"Unsure at the moment. But proceed with caution. Novac is unstable. I'll have units on the scene ASAP—over and out."

Marcus checked his map and found Dribble Creek Drive easily. It was at the edge of town alright. Right in the upper corner just under the mine which shared its name. He checked the chamber of his pistol, loaded it, and put the car in drive.

27

ARTIE
THE DISCOVERY…

THE CORRIDOR WAS wet and cold, and with every few steps Artie took, icy water would splash up from a puddle to touch his legs as he followed the tiny creatures through the winding mine tunnels. Martin's lighter had been especially useful, as random rocks from the tunnel ceiling jutted out every now and then, threatening to smack him square in the face if he wasn't careful. The creatures had no need to worry about this. The tallest of them went up to about Artie's knee, and the smaller ones were no more than a foot tall. They moved through the tunnels with ease, barely even bumping into or walking on top of one another.

Artie's back continued to hurt with him hunched over. He hadn't been able to stand up straight since he awakened to find the tiny creatures surrounding him. How long it had been since then Artie could not say, and he had abandoned counting his footsteps after 250, which for all he knew could have been 1,000 steps ago by now.

He held the lighter out in front of his face, merely inches from the tunnel ceiling. And twice now he'd heard a small *pop* come from the space between his lighter and the ceiling, like someone had punctured a small balloon.

He'd heard of methane build up in mines before, but he'd never experienced it himself. And from what he heard from miners in the town, it was, for the most part, harmless. Besides, he needed the light to see. The darkness was more treacherous —and terrifying—than any little burst of flame.

When the tiny creatures rounded the next corner, they dispersed wider than Artie could see. And when he himself rounded the corner, the light from the flame he was holding shone wider, reaching out to touch a more open expanse of darkness, and Artie was relieved to step into a clearing in the rock formation and finally stand up straight.

He stretched his back and moved the light around to see the walls of the cave. Little streams of water ran down the sides from the cavernous ceiling that was at least twice as tall as Artie was standing full. The light couldn't even extend to the far side wall —if there was a wall—and Artie watched as the tiny creatures continued to scatter about throughout the open ground before him.

But as he moved his light around inspecting the cave, his relief turned to dread. For he could hear, from somewhere, unmistakably, the soft swinging of the rope. Back and forth. Back and forth. And it echoed softly from all around him. He stumbled forward trying to spot it. To the right, to the left, behind him, there was nothing but cave walls. He walked forward to the dark and still hidden section of the cave, the rhythmic aching of the rope still quietly singing its tune.

Looking up, he could see nothing but the shimmering reflection of water running down the walls. Then his foot caught something, and he stumbled forward, causing his light to go out. When he regained himself, he rested on his knees and could feel some kind of soft, fluffy fabric on the ground next to him. He flicked his lighter again. Laying before him was a dark blue lump. It was much bigger than he was, and it wasn't until Artie got to his feet that he realized what he was looking at. It was the rounded body of a man wearing nothing but his underwear and a bathrobe the color of blue velvet. The robe was missing the right sleeve at the shoulder, and it looked as if the arm that should have been inside was missing as well.

A few of the tiny creatures scampered by, climbing over the fat man's stomach and disappearing again. One even appeared to go *inside* the man's stomach. Artie took a step back and felt the heel of his foot hit something hard. He turned and moved his light to the ground to see a pair of muddy work boots laying on their heels. He followed the legs connected to the boots up to the torso to find another body, large, but not quite as big as the one in the bathrobe, laying up against the wall. The stomach had been opened, and from the looks of it, gutted clean out. Artie could see the lining of the man's stomach surrounding an empty and organ-less cave, a macabre replica of the one he himself was standing in. On the outside of the open stomach Artie saw the body was wearing a brown and tattered leather jacket. One that he knew he had seen before. He used his lighter to follow the jacket up the arms to the shoulders that sat against the stone wall of the cave. That was it. Just shoulders. This body had no head, and at that moment Artie realized he was standing over the decapitated body of Dave Meyrowitz.

28

ARTIE

HE'S HERE...

HIS OWN BREATH had put the light out. And now Artie struggled to flick the lighter again, his hand trembling, his heart racing. He could still hear the haunting swinging of the rope. *That goddamn fucking rope.*

When he was finally able to get his light source back, Artie examined Dave's body further. It was headless, and it was Dave. No doubt about it. He was almost relieved. As relieved as he could be in a situation like this. He even let out a nervous bit of laughter. "I'm not crazy... I'm not crazy after all. He's here, you fucking fools. He's *here!*" Artie shouted to no one. His voice echoed loudly off the walls. *"he's here he's here he's here..."*

Artie took a step back and shone his light deeper into the darkness. He walked past the two bodies of the fat men and heard a crunching sound beneath his feet. Littered throughout the cave floor, like wildflowers in a meadow, was a garden of bones. Some human—Artie could see human skulls, maybe half a dozen of them, a few femurs, some hand bones, one curled around a rosary, the silver crucifix reflected off Artie's lighter—some not human; right next to his foot was the skull and antlers of a deer. And some *almost* human... For there was the strangest looking skull Artie had ever seen laying on its side against the far wall. It was shaped like a human skull, but it was twice the size, with an elongated crowning of the head. The jaw bones were wide and the teeth that remained inside were long and fierce. If there were other much-too-large bones to accompany this gargantuan head, Artie could not see them.

But he could see clothing scattered, most of it rotted, decaying, following the path of its once wearers. An orange hunting jacket... A pair of tattered jeans... A pink and silver backpack...

Then his eye caught a navy-blue jumpsuit. The skeleton still inside of it. Artie approached it, crouched down, and brought his lighter close to the patch on the left breast pocket. It read *B. Novac*, and Artie lowered his head.

So, he was right about that too, he thought to himself, tears beginning to swell in his eyes. This validation, however, did not bring the relief Artie was expecting. Instead, it brought him waves of sorrow and anger.

"I knew it," he said quietly. "I told 'em, Pop. I told 'em you didn't leave me." Artie touched the back of his father's skull, held it gently, and continued to cry. He began to mumble a soft prayer, reciting the "Our Father" as best he could.

"Save your prayers for the living," a voice said softly from behind him. Artie stood, turned, and shone his light. There stood his father, fully nude, and sickly thin. His skin was a ghostly white, nearly transparent.

Artie wiped his tears away with the back of his hand. "Pop," he said. "You're alive."

"Far from it." The ghost extended its thin white arms out to the side and gestured to the cave. "What a cruel life this would be." Artie gazed around the cave again briefly. Piles of bones, dripping water, and the tiny creatures moving about. "Though not as cruel as yours, I suppose."

"What do you mean, Pop?"

"Can you not tell? You're cursed, Arthur. Haunted. Though not by spirits..."

After his father said this, the cave grew even quieter. As if the dripping water had dried up. Artie realized he couldn't even hear the rope. "I—I don't understand."

"It's my fault, really."

Artie took a step closer. "Don't say that—"

"Don't come any closer!" The ghost ordered. "It's true. I gave you this curse. And to your mother. Though her curse was physical...

"I'm drawn to this place, son. Just like you were. I was even warned, decades ago, by an Indian who knew its secrets." It motioned to the cave again.

"What place?" Artie asked.

"The ancients have used this cave system for millions of years. I never would have believed it. But I've been witness to it now for a long time. This is not a place for men, Arthur. We should never have dug here."

"Why did you?"

The ghost paused for a moment. Then spoke. "Because we were paid to, I suppose. After all, what more could I have provided in a place like this...

"But there's more than coal in this mine, Arthur. I discovered the silver deposits myself. Me and my team tried to keep it a secret. We had to. If the coal company found out, they'd harvest it all for themselves.

"But there was more than silver down here, too. We found that out the hard way."

Artie scratched the back of his head. "So I'm not crazy then!? I was right about you dying in here."

The ghost laughed a hollow, horrific laugh. "You think madness is sudden? A little man shows up one day to tinker around in your brain, flicking switches and pulling levers? It isn't flicking switches and pulling levers, Arthur. It's a hundred tiny incisions; snipping wires and slicing the walls of your brain as the innards ooze down through tiny, maze-like passages that make up your mind, taking the fabric of reality along with it."

Artie touched his head again. It was beginning to hurt. His father had never spoken like this when he was alive. Perhaps there is eloquence in death, he thought. Or maybe those incisions were working, and the wires of his brain were hanging on by a thread. Or worse, already severed.

"Are you even real?" Artie asked.

The ghost shrugged. "Do I have to be? Or have I made my point all the same?"

Artie opened his mouth to respond, but the ghost of his father cut him off. "Enough talk. You're wasting time. Have you forgotten why you came here?" It pointed to the far back corner of the cave, "This one still looks to be alive."

Artie shone the lighter to where the ghost was pointing, and, sure enough, he saw another lump on the ground. This one smaller than the other two, wearing a stained silver jacket. He walked over and noticed the lump was moving slowly, breathing quietly, though unconscious. Dirty blond hair covered the face, and Artie brushed it with his hand. Theo Meyrowitz was alive, and from what Artie could tell, mostly unharmed.

He looked back to speak to his father again, but the specter was gone.

"Glad that creep finally left." Artie heard a different, hoarse voice say.

Dave's head was tucked behind where his daughter was laying.

"There you are," Artie said.

"Yeah yeah. Here I am. Now, get my girl the Hell out of this place."

29

MARCUS
I'VE BEEN WAITING...

Marcus was the first to arrive at the end of Dribble Creek Drive. He parked at the end of the road in front of the house on the corner. How he'd beaten the rest of the Sheriff's police force to the scene, he couldn't be sure. But slow responders are slow responders. Marcus had learned that the hard way back in Baltimore.

The moment he turned off the ignition and opened his car door, a woman burst out of the corner house and ran up to him. She was clearly frazzled, eyes red with tears, blonde hair frizzy and unkept.

"Where's the cops?" she asked. "I called them over 15 minutes ago."

Marcus exited his vehicle and shut the door. "I'm an officer, ma'am. What's the problem?"

"I told them already; my daughter's been kidnapped!" She pointed behind the house to the woods across the field.

"I'm on it, ma'am," Marcus said as he holstered his pistol. He pointed to the house. "I need you to get back inside and wait for the rest of the officers."

"I've been waitin'!" she cried. "Oh God, my poor baby."

Marcus saw a young girl standing in the open doorway of the woman's house. "Ma'am, please. Go back inside and lock your door. Let us handle this."

"Hurry then! That fucking *monster* took her!" She pointed again aggressively to the woods behind the house.

Marcus left the woman standing in the yard and began running at a full sprint through the field. "Go back inside!" he shouted to the woman as he ran, cutting through the wildflowers and tall grasses, his face and hands receiving small cuts from thorns as he went.

It was almost surreal. He was running through a field. The sun shining brightly. Grasshoppers and other insects jumping out of his way as he trampled over blades of grass that were up to his hips. Birds flying above him. The only sounds were the *swish swish* of his body through the meadow and his own heartbeat thumping loudly in his ears.

He was a far cry from the city streets he used to run through as a boy, but the feeling was familiar. A panic fueled ecstasy. Except instead of running from danger—a street corner exodus at the sign of a cop or the frantic dispersal after a wayward gunshot—he was running *toward* it.

The entrance to the mine was obvious. It sat in a clearing at the edge of the field, tucked into the hill where an enormous and dark forest loomed ominously behind it. Marcus stopped to catch his breath at the mouth of the tunnel. He bent over, placing his hands on his knees and tried to steady his breathing. Looking behind him, he could see the little neighborhood on the far side of the field he'd just run through. No backup yet...

Marcus turned back toward the mine entrance and stood up straight. He took his pistol in his right hand and checked the chamber again. Loaded. He took his flashlight in his left hand and turned it on, shining it into the pitch-black mouth of the tunnel.

At the base of the entrance, Marcus could see a kind of white clay that was soft like fresh mud. And there were dozens of tiny three-pronged footprints embedded in the ground that led into the tunnel. Then he noticed a set of larger, fresh-looking boot prints that also went into the dark.

He shook his head. If only the boys in Baltimore could see him now. And with that thought, Marcus began his descent into the Dribble Creek Colliery.

30

ARTIE

THAT'S THE DIFFERENCE...

ARTIE GATHERED the girl's body as best he could and sat her upright against the wall of the cave. Her head slumped down toward her chest, and she was snoring quietly.

Dave's head floated up to Artie and faced his daughter. "I told ya not to come down here, Artie."

"Mhm," Artie said, gently tapping the girl's face with his hand. "Theo. Can you hear me? Wake up." He tapped her cheek a few more times.

"At least she might have chance now, I guess," the head said. "But it's over for you. And that means it's over for me too."

"Is that so?" Artie looked at Dave. The floating head had an unlit cigarette in its mouth. "Guess your lucks run out then," he said.

"My luck ran out a long time ago," the head said quietly. "Say, Artie. Can I get a light?"

Artie was still holding the lighter in his left hand, his right hand holding up Theo by the shoulder. He moved the lighter to the cigarette between Dave's teeth. The dismembered head inhaled, and the cherry of the cigarette caught.

"Thanks, kid." Dave exhaled smoke that spiraled up to the

cavern ceiling. "Seems like just yesterday we were havin' beers, talkin' shit." The head laughed.

Artie smiled and nodded, but didn't laugh.

"I know it ain't been easy on ya. Giving your folks passing and all," said Dave. "But you got a helluva rage built up in you."

"Thanks... I guess"

"Ya done good lettin' it out, too. Shit'll kill ya if it builds up too much, ya know."

Artie laughed sarcastically. "So you were just looking out for me, huh?" He tapped the girl's face again and she began to stir, moving her head to the side.

"You're damn right I was," Dave said, exhaling more smoke into the air. "Gotta admit it was kinda fun though, heh?" He chuckled.

"Speak for yourself," Artie said. "Come on, Theo. We need to get you out of here." She mumbled something but didn't wake up.

"Well, shit, I had fun," said Dave. "Plus, I made sure you ain't got caught, didn't I?"

"I see," said Artie. "Guess you've been my guardian angel of sorts, huh?"

The head laughed a quiet, sorrowful laugh. "That's the difference between angels and demons, Artie. Angels stay in heaven."

Then the girl coughed slightly and began to open her eyes. She squinted at the flame from Artie's lighter and took a few moments to awaken fully. She shook her head and coughed again. "Daddy?" she said. "Is that you?"

Artie looked behind him, but Dave's head was nowhere to be found. "Hey Theo, it's me. Arthur. Your Dad's friend. We gotta get—"

But as Artie was talking the girl's eyes became wide and frightened. They were looking past Artie, over his shoulder above him. Then she let out a shrill cry of terror. And as Artie turned around, he saw two burning red eyes perched atop the cave ceiling. And the next thing he knew, the eyes fell toward him in an instant, then stood merely inches away from his own, and Artie could smell the hot, putrid breath of the creature he'd seen just days ago, atop the cemetery hill.

31

MARCUS

THE FOLLOWING II...

THE FLASHLIGHT the Sheriff had given him was weak, and Marcus could hardly see 10 feet in front of him in the thick and swallowing darkness of the mine tunnel. He'd fully entered the tunnel about five minutes ago, but he found he hadn't gone very far. Every few steps he looked back over his shoulder at the light that shone like a tiny, bright sun in the encompassing black space that was the cave. And the sun was shrinking the further he crept.

He'd been following the boot prints like breadcrumbs, even though he'd been walking in a straight, narrow line the whole time. The boot prints were nearly stacked on top of one another, as whosoever they were had been walking even slower than shorter gaited that Marcus was.

The air was getting increasingly colder, and Marcus could now see his breath in the light of his flashlight, protruding out from him like the spectral mist of destiny, leading him ever forward down his path of darkness. For a drift mine, this tunnel had a rather steep decline, almost to the degree of a slope mine, though far less intense than the well known shaft mines that require a crude looking elevator to descend. Marcus was thankful this was *not* a shaft mine. For no matter how much danger a young girl was in, Marcus doubted even he would have the balls to close the gate on rusted metal box and ride the rickety thing down to the depths of the Earth's core.

No. Walking would suffice. And walking slowly, at that...

After some time, the tiny sun behind him had shrunk to a while dwarf star, barely visible and far, far away. The air was colder still, and the only sounds were the drips of icy water falling from the cave ceiling and the faint echoes they left behind. Marcus shuttered and cast his light ahead of him. But only a few steps further, and Marcus paused. The tiny footprints from various, unknown animals continued, but the boot prints had stopped dead. Just vanished, as if whoever had made them turned into a ghost and floated onward. He cast his flashlight behind him, on the walls, the ceiling, but there was no visible backtracking or any other sign of human evidence.

He was puzzled, and then Marcus heard something that was unmistakable, yet impossible. A sound that caused him to hold his breath and stand still, every single hair on his body standing straight up.

There was the quiet, subtle sound of a baby crying in the distance. A high-pitched wailing that seemed to come from the dark tunnel within. It lasted for maybe five seconds, but the echo it left seemed to stretch on for minutes. Down and down, repeated again and again, each time a little quieter but never softer. Never any less shrill.

When it finally passed, Marcus let out his breath, and with it, an involuntary whimper. He was shaking, and the light from his flashlight bounced over the walls in jittery, sudden movements. His first instinct was to run. Scamper back into the warm summer sun with his tail between his legs. But he didn't. He stood still. He was alone and far from home, but a little girl needed his help. And he'd faced tougher things than some hillbilly psycho hiding in a cave mine. He'd gone toe to toe with some of the most ruthless gangsters in the country... Ones who flayed their rivals just for the fun of it... Ones that operated practically in his own backyard... Compared to that, how scary could a baby be?

32

ARTIE

THE LIGHT...

HIS FIRST INSTINCT was to run. Run forever like a deer that's just been shot at. But he found his feet wouldn't move. So, Artie was forced into his second instinct: to fight.

The creature stood in front of Artie. Towering over him, the wings on its shoulders nearly touching the cave ceiling. Its face was lower, and Artie took the Zippo lighter in his left hand, snapped it shut, and the cave went dark. But Artie could still see the afterglow of the creature's giant red eyes. So, he took his fist, lighter clenched within, and propelled it with all his might into the thing's left eye.

The creature gave a slight grunt, then Artie felt something hit his side with such force that he was thrown into the wall. His face smacked the cave rock, and he collapsed holding his torso.

It was hard to breathe, he felt as if his lungs had been deflated. He coughed, and that hurt even more. He thought he might hack up a chunk of lung or maybe a piece of rib that had broken off, tumbling about inside of him.

He was laying with his cheek to the ground, curled up like a beat dog. It was pitch black, and the sound of his ragged breathing was quickly replaced with something much louder:

the panicked screeches of a girl in distress. Then Artie heard some kind of high-pitched hissing and clicking sounds coming from the same corner, and he heard the scratching of the creature's claws moving across the stone floor.

The horrible sounds of the girl's screaming and the creature's hissing filled the cave and echoed down the tunnels in a cacophony of horror.

It was easier to lie there. Even easier to just sleep. To let the overwhelming feeling of drowning—suffocating—fill him to the brink. If he died right here, perhaps he'd live on like a specter the way his father had. At least that would make a better ghost than one his mother's memory had become. One that haunts an old home; a little piece of soul stuck in the drywall of some family's living room or basement. *Such a terrible thing.* He'd felt more like a ghost than a human the last few days anyway. Maybe it was time to commit.

"Oh God, please no," Artie heard the girl sob. And her cry awoken something familiar in him. The girl sounded almost exactly like her mother. And through the pitch black, Artie could see Carol's face in tears. The muffled cries for help as her daughter struggled to fight off a thing once only found in her nightmares.

Struggling, Artie got on his hands and knees. He began to cough viciously to the point of wheezing. And when he thought he'd coughed up all the blood he had in his body, he vomited whatever bile was left in his stomach. Emaciated as he was, there wasn't much to throw up. So, he got to his feet. The girl was still crying and screaming, and Artie followed the sounds of her struggling.

He stumbled his way to the sounds of commotion, and when he was close, he flicked his lighter on to see the creature standing before the girl, its right arm reaching back, long claws extending from the thing's hand. With all the effort he had left,

Artie lunged toward the girl, and when the creature struck, its claw hit him in the stomach, and he felt a piercing sensation that was hot and cold at the same time. He clenched his fist, and the light was put out.

The next few moments were a blur, and Artie was fading in and out of consciousness. It was like those early morning dreams when the sunlight shines through the curtain just enough to walk the sleeper on the tightrope of dream and reality. He felt his body rising, stuck horizontally in the air like a piece of meat on a kabob. And his stomach where he felt the piercing was burning and wet. Then he heard the sound of laughter, loud and ecstatic, bouncing all around him. He was being raised up higher and higher, and when the creature brought his limp body up to its face near the ceiling of the cave, Artie used the last of his energy to flick the lighter once more.

THE LIGHT WAS the last thing he remembered. Not the fire, not the sound of the explosion. Just the light, emanating from his fist like a flamethrower. Like the atomic bomb testing he'd seen on TV. That magnificent power in his small hand, blasted straight into the face of terror before him.

But everything after that was dull. He couldn't see. He couldn't hear. He couldn't feel anything. But he would always remember the light.

33

MARCUS

HIDE AND SEEK...

SINCE HE'D HEARD the sound of the baby crying, Marcus had been hyperaware of his own sounds... His short and heavy breathing... His small and cautious footsteps... The incessant ringing of his ears when all seem *too* quiet...

Everything was too quiet now. And every sound was far too loud. The dripping from the ceiling moved him along like a drum beat; another soldier marching to the rhythm of certain peril. God, what he wouldn't give to be back on that beach in North Carolina. Letting the sun soak his skin and hold him in a warm embrace of content. He didn't suppose there was a further thing from that place right now. And all the while, the dripping continued.

The tunnel Marcus walked through now was getting smaller. The walls on either side were tightening, and his head was nearly touching the top of the ceiling. He'd given up looking for more boot prints, keeping his eyes intensely fixed upon the shrinking tunnel before him.

He was reminded of a game he used to play with his cousins as a child. "Hide and seek in the dark" they called it. The game, while unoriginally named, was exactly what it sounded like: All

the cousins would turn off the lights in the basement, put blan-
kets on the windows, and hide amongst the piles of laundry,
coffee tables, cardboard boxes, whatever could be used as a kind
of barricade. Then the seeker would slink around the room
listening for any sound of movement or breathing. Using their
hands to feel their way around the dark, sometimes shouting
BOO! at an empty space hoping to frighten one of the hiders into
shrieking.

Marcus had enjoyed this game very much. But with all the
excitement it caused, a great amount of fear came with it. They
were children playing in a safe place, where they knew no harm
would befall them. But there was something about the sheer
darkness of the room and the quiet waiting and stifling of breath
that created a sense of restless terror and anxiety. Marcus would
almost always give away his hiding position if the seeker got too
close to him. When he could hear hands tapping on the nearby
walls, or the rustling of footsteps in front of him, or even the hot
breath of the seeker merely inches from his own face, Marcus
couldn't help but let out an enormous fit of nervous laughter. He
would try with all his might to hold it in. He'd tell himself the
next time they played that he would bite his lip so hard he'd
make himself bleed if he had to. But it was no use. When he felt
he was about to be discovered in the dark, he simply could not
contain his laughter. He felt like laughing now... An uncontrol-
lable sense to laugh even though there was nothing fun nor
funny about this situation.

But nonetheless, the sensation was building. As he ducked
down to keep his head from hitting the ceiling, he tried biting
his lip to hold back the laugh. His breathing became faster, and
he could feel the laughter building in his belly. Then, he knew
there was no stopping it. He let out a roar of nervous laughter.
So full and heavy that he doubled over and stood hunched with
his hands on his knees just bellowing out. He laughed so hard

he began to cry. And the booming echo of his laughter carried throughout the tunnel.

Finally, when he was able to get ahold of himself, he wiped the tears from his eyes and shook his head. He stood up as far as he could and shined his flashlight forward. He took one step then... *BOOM!*

There was the thundering sound of a tremendous explosion, followed by the rush and wave of wind that hit Marcus in the face so hard he had to close his eyes until it passed. The tunnel floor shook briefly, forcing Marcus to brace himself with both his arms pressed hard against the walls. It had come from in front of him. And whatever it was, it didn't sound good.

Moving quickly now, he hurried forward. It was hard to see for sure being hunched over the way he was, but it looked as if his flashlight touched on an opening ahead. He rushed forward and squeezed through the tightest part of the tunnel yet, leading him into what he guessed was the open expanse of a cave, though all his flashlight was illuminating was dust and smoke, floating lazily upward, billowing like a mushroom cloud.

34

THE COLLECTION...

HE TOOK one deep breath and hit the deck. The air was thick with smoke and ash and Marcus coughed into his sleeve as he got down of all fours, then he loosened his tie and brought his shirt up to cover his mouth. It was slightly clearer down on the ground, so Marcus used his flashlight to look around. At first, he thought he might be looking at the replica of a small town. Perhaps a model of Jerusalem with an expanse of sedimentary limestone buildings under a shroud of mist above. In a way, that would make him God, peering down from the clouds at the unexpecting and disinterested town below. But as more smoke cleared, Marcus realized that he wasn't looking at a small town, but a burial ground; littered with bones that were scattered across the floor. There were smaller bones, and there were bigger bones. There were some he recognized (like a human skull), and some he didn't (like a... *what would you call that?*). Then his light hit something toward the far end of the room that sparkled in the light. Whatever it was moved again, and Marcus heard a faint crying and coughing sound come from that way.

Still on his hands and knees, Marcus lowered his shirt

exposing his mouth, and put his flashlight in between his teeth. Then he began to crawl forward.

There was a small path cleared already, but Marcus had to brush aside dozens of bones that lay in his way as he went. Between small coughing fits that jutted the flashlight in his mouth, he was on the brink of another nervous bout of laughter. But the laughing led to more coughing, and he was soon overcome with aggressive hacking that caused him to stop about halfway to the shimmering mound that was moving about every so often.

Marcus caught his breath as best he could and continued crawling forward until he reached the outstretched and naked legs of a man in a blue bathrobe. There, he stopped and examined the body with his flashlight. The man was dead alright. How recently, Marcus couldn't be sure. But the flesh wasn't decayed, and the only thing he could smell was sulfur and dust. He continued, and a few paces later came across another leg sprawled out to his left. This one was clothed at least and wearing a boot on the foot. Marcus shined his flashlight over the body and noticed it was sitting up with its back against the wall. The smoke cloud was thick above the man's shoulders, but Marcus could tell he wasn't breathing, for his large stomach, like the man in bathrobe, was not moving in and out struggling for air.

There was the sound of soft coughing again from in front of him, and Marcus saw the shimmering light reflected off the source of the noise. It was a bedazzled pink jacket that *was* clearly moving in and out. He approached it, still crawling, and reached his hand out to touch it. When he did, the girl screamed and pushed his hand off her.

"Hey, it's okay. I got you," Marcus said gently. He touched the girl's shoulder again and turned her around to face him. The first thing he saw were strands of blonde hair covering half of the girl's face, some frayed and singed, some still intact. But the other half of the girl's face had been burnt badly, and pink flesh hung from her right cheek. Her right eye and right ear were badly burnt as well, and the hair on the right side of her head from her temple to behind her ear was completely gone.

The girl made a quivering noise when Marcus touched her arm. "It's okay," he said again. She cried quietly, and Marcus shined his flashlight into her left eye. It wasn't burnt, but it was glazed over, not reacting at all to his light. "Can you see me?" he asked. No response. "Here," he said, trying to gather the girl to her feet. "Can you walk?"

She shook her head and cried again. "Okay. Come on." He stood up, his head now completely covered in smoke. "I got you," he said as he tried to lift the girl into his arms. She was heavier than she looked, and Marcus struggled to bring her limp body off the ground. When he finally got her to her feet, she crumbled and fell back down to her knees. Marcus joined her, getting down on his knees and keeping his head below the cloud of smoke that was still rising and convulsing in the cave.

The girl touched her face and winced in pain. "What's happened to me?" she cried.

Marcus put his hand on her shoulder and squeezed. "It's alright now. But we have to get out of here."

"B—But. He's... there." She pointed behind Marcus. Her one good eye alive again, fueled intensely by some unknown horror. Above him, over his shoulder she pointed. Marcus turned and looked around with the flashlight but couldn't see anything except smoke.

He crouched again and shined his light on the ground toward the back corner of the cave. There was something on the ground. He left the girl on her knees and crawled over to the corner. There, huddled against the wall, was the burnt husk of a body. The only fabric seemingly unsinged was a square foot patch of flannel on the back of the body. Smoke still rose from the corpse, and any sign of identification had been melted away. *Here lies the monster*, Marcus thought. He felt his stomach turn, and he felt a desire to shoot it, just to be sure. He thought about the diner girl in the alley, and almost got sick right there. Instead, he swallowed it, and turned back toward the girl.

"It's okay, he can't hurt you now." He gathered the girl again and they both stood. She was leaning on him as they walked. Marcus was practically dragging her by the time they passed the bodies of the large men on the ground. He nearly tripped when he caught the boot of the dead man. Catching himself and the girl, Marcus let out a series of brutal coughs that turned to laughter toward the end. The girl mumbled something that Marcus didn't quite hear... Something with the word "boots"...

Using his flashlight, he scanned the room. There were many tunnels that led to this opening, so Marcus had to check the entrance to each one for his footprints to find his way out. He approached the first opening with the girl still on his shoulder. He crouched down under the smoke to examine the ground. Nothing. Then he came to the second opening. Still nothing. But when he came to the third opening, he didn't see his footprints, but instead, a faint light coming from the other side...

He crouched down on his knees to get a better look, bringing the girl down with him. He poked his head through and stared in disbelief. He was looking at a circular archway, swirling like a far-off galaxy comprised of more colors than he could recognize; colors he didn't know existed. They spiraled outward from the center, and Marcus could feel some kind of warmth emanating from the colors. He was mesmerized; stunned by its beauty. There were noises coming from it. Like static, or if sparkling had a sound, he thought.

It wasn't much bigger than he was, but its sheer presence made Marcus feel... small... insignificant... like nothing he had ever done had mattered... even this rescue mission he was on... it was useless... pointless... He was drooling, in a complete trance, and then the girl fell and hit the ground with a thud.

Marcus shook his head and blinked his eyes. "Shit," he said, then he scooped the girl up and turned back into the bigger room. "Sorry about that." But the girl was unconscious.

He used his flashlight again to check for more tunnel openings. When he was finally able to retrace his steps and find the small opening to the tunnel he'd come in through, he gently pushed the girl through first. He then turned back toward the center of the cave and stood upright, stretching his back before the long, hunched journey through the tunnels that he knew lay ahead of him. He held his breath in the smoke and shined his light once more around the cave. He must have been hallucinating due to a lack of oxygen intake, because before he entered the tunnel to continue on with the girl, Marcus could swear he saw, in the thickness of the billowing smoke, two tall, ghostly white figures from head to toe, arms extended, as if longing for an embrace.

35

WALKING TOWARD THE LIGHT...

THE JOURNEY out of the mine was a blur. Marcus had led the way as best he could, trying to recall the path he'd taken on his way in. But the tunnels were so tight at some places, that he ended up dragging the poor injured girl behind him as he went. He was exhausted, and he was sick. The smoke inhalation had caused him to vomit so many times that eventually he didn't even stop, he simply threw up whatever bile was left in him down his shirt and kept walking. The girl was unconscious for most of it, and every few minutes, Marcus would shine his flashlight on her long enough to see her chest move, then continue dragging her along by the feet.

He was reminded again of days in his youth, running for his life in the streets of the city. "Don't stop," he told himself. He didn't know where he was going nor for how long he'd have to run but... "Never stop."

His head was woozy, and more than a few times, he'd nearly keeled over and passed out. He was seeing things, too. He imagined he saw dozens of little white rabbits leading him through the tunnels. He shook his head violently and squinted his eyes a few times, but the rabbits always seemed to disappear.

After some time, Marcus had no idea how long, he began to see a light at the end of the tunnel. When he did, it became like a beacon of hope. They were almost out. Marcus wondered if the old wives' tale was true, and perhaps he was indeed *walking toward the light* at the end of the tunnel that was, itself, his own life. Though, he supposed, whatever awaited him at the light he was headed for was better than being in the tunnel itself. So, barely conscious, barely breathing, he continued.

When he neared the end of the tunnel, Marcus saw shapes and shadows emerging from the light. There was a rustling of feet and voices, and even the sound of some far off, distant applause. The air was hot and fresh again, and like seeing a lover that's been away for too long, he collapsed into the warm embrace of the long-awaited sunlight.

EPILOGUE

THE COFFEE WAS BITTER, so Clyde added two spoonsful of cream and swirled it around until the black liquid turned light brown. He took another sip. Too sweet. Reaching into the bottom right drawer of his desk, Clyde pulled out a handle of Jameson, poured some into his mug, and sipped it. *Getting there*, he thought. He added a bit more, then tasted it again. *There we go.*

He set his mug down on a stack of papers with the word CONFIDENTIAL written diagonally across them in big red letters. He'd just finished reading the report, but the conclusion was baffling. Standing up from his desk, he turned and faced the window, looking out onto the busy street of Pennsylvania Avenue on another bright, summer morning.

He was watching a young woman walking her dog. It was a tiny thing, perhaps a puppy, and Clyde watched as it squatted and did its business on the sidewalk across the street. *Hope she brought a bag for that*, he thought. But before he could confirm whether or not the woman did indeed clean up her pet's mess, there was a knock on his office door. Then it opened.

"Sir?" said a man's voice through the crack in the door.

"Come in," Clyde responded.

"You wanted to see me, sir?"

Clyde turned back toward his desk. "Close the door, Sam."

The young man wearing a black suit much like Clyde's shut the door and approached the desk. "Deputy Director," he said.

"Sit down," said Clyde, and motioned Sam to the chair on the other side of the desk. He moved his coffee mug to the side and picked up the stack of papers. "What do you make of this?" He slammed the papers down on the desk again.

The color in Sam's face went pale. "Well, sir. It—er—appears that—that the fatal bullet may indeed have come from the vehicle directly behind the President's." Sam looked down at the desk.

Clyde didn't say anything. He merely continued to stand, placed both hands on the desk in front of him, and lowered his head.

"It was surely accidental, sir," added Sam.

"Goddamn CIA," said Clyde. "Fucking morons."

"Yes, sir," Sam said quietly.

"Don't let Lyndon find out about this."

"Yes sir."

"Matter of fact," Clyde picked up the papers. "Bury it." He handed them to Sam. "And destroy these. The embarrassment this would cause if it got out..." Clyde shook his head.

"Yes sir," said Sam. He took the papers, stood up, and headed for the office door.

"Not a word of this, Sam. To anyone."

Sam nodded and opened the door.

As Sam exited the office, another man in a suit, this one older and tougher looking, with a thick mustache and glasses poked his head through the door.

"Deputy Director," the man said in a deep, rough voice, "if you have a moment."

"What is it, Curtis?"

The man entered the office and shut the door behind him. "Well sir, just wanted to give you an update on the Burnwell case."

Clyde sat back down in his chair. "The what now?"

The man with the mustache cleared his throat. "The—uh—disturbance in West Virgina, sir."

Clyde just looked at him.

"With the—uh—cave system," he said quietly.

Clyde took a sip of coffee. "Ah. Yes. What about it?"

"Well sir, mission complete. No harm done."

"Any witnesses?"

"None alive, sir."

"And the... *anomaly*?"

"Still open, as you requested. The mine entrance has been boarded shut, but it won't be flooded."

"Good," Clyde said. He took another sip of coffee. "What's the official report?"

"Local lunatic on a murderous rampage," the man said. "Made sure all the papers say so."

"How about our boy?"

"Wrathmore, sir. Good kid. Either he doesn't remember much, or he's smart enough to play it that way. But he's recovering."

"Well done. See that the kid gets his vacation back when he's well."

"Yes sir."

"Oh," said Clyde. "What about our local guy?"

The man shrugged. "The Sheriff knows the deal. He keeps things pretty tight down there. Got a real foothold in that community."

Clyde took another sip of coffee and sighed. "Alright then, Curtis. Good work."

The man stood up. "Should we tell the Director?" he said.

"I wouldn't bother J. about this," Clyde said. "He had a rather —long night. Bigger fish to fry and all that." He waved his hand nonchalantly.

"Of course, sir," said the man, and he headed for the door.

ABOUT THE AUTHOR

Michael Schussler Jr. was born and raised in Silver Run, Maryland, where the fields and streams spoke whispers to him in an unknown, ancient tongue. Try as he might to capture their stories, he admits that he understands very little. To take magic from the air and translate it into words is — as he puts it — "Impossible... but worth every moment." His poems and stories have appeared in several literary magazines. He's worked as a sports journalist and analyst, a ghostwriter (not that kind), and as a managing editor for a variety of publications.

Made in United States
Orlando, FL
02 March 2024

44297196R00085